Touched

L. G. Boyle

For MaDear:

When I was a little girl you told me I could do and be anything. Only now am I starting to believe.

With eternal gratitude and thanks:

To my daughter, Loreah – at one point I worked to become your (s)hero, and now you have become mine. I'm so very proud of you! To my son, Larrie, my web designer and consultant on all things having to do with this virtual age. You pushed, poked and prodded me until I finished my manuscript. You inspired me and made me believe, again. To my sister, Norvella (and her family), you are my friend, confidante, secretary extraordinaire, my biggest supporter and the best part of my retinue. To my brother, George, for the times you've spent infusing me with your knowledge and our many talks that went way into the night. To my brother Jerry, for your occasional, genuine nuggets of wisdom that stay with me.

Acknowledgements

To Phyllis, Valerie and Brenda, for the parts you've played in my evolution to become an author – thank you! To Sharon W – when I confessed I wanted to write a book, you simply said, "Why don't you?" To my G'Pa Dwight, for all my outdoor scenes – anything done well comes from him. All errors are my own! To the Reverends Freelon and Tabb, who have supported my various ministries and first called me "author." To Rev. Jason, who merely said, "Can I read it?" To the Falcons, my classmates, for saving me from bearing the full brunt of empty nest syndrome and providing so many great memories. To my BDG, friends, family, church families and Word in My Life readers (hereafter known as "Wordies") too numerous to name, this book was made possible by your love, support and encouragement.

Foreword

First time author, L. G. Boyle, makes an awesome debut in "Touched." A gifted writer and learned Bible Study leader, Boyle uses biblical knowledge and divine genius to weave together a wonderful Christian fiction that inspires the reader to walk in the supernatural power that the Bible promises all believers.

Isaiah 45:1 says "...concerning the work of my hands command ye me." Students of the Bible know that it is chocked full of amazing stories of individuals who commanded the work of God's hands and, therefore, demonstrated the supernatural power of God: Moses held out his rod and God split the Red Sea; Joshua prayed and God stopped the sun and the moon to lengthen the day; Elijah prayed and God stopped the rain for three years and six months – he prayed again and the rain began; Jesus prayed over five loaves and two fish and fed more than 5000, with leftovers. The list of miracles goes on and on....

Let "Touched" entice you to become child-like before God not unlike Mal, Ari and Martha—the fascinating characters in "Touched"—and command the work of God's hands to overcome challenges in our lives, communities, nations and the world. "Touched" keeps the reader in suspense about the next amazing miracle that Mal, Ari and Martha might perform as they walk in the supernatural powers bestowed upon them by the Young Master.

This pleasing and easy to read book is for all age groups - children, youth and adults alike. It is ideal for group readings to compare and contrast to the actual Bible stories that inspired this body of work by L. G. Boyle. We wait with bated breath for the next installment of tales of the supernatural powers demonstrated by Mal, Ari and Martha.

Rev. Atty. Sheila Wilson-Freelon, Mdiv
~Senior Pastor, Turner Memorial AME Church
~Evangelism Director, SD and Chairperson,
Chicago Annual Conference AME Church

"Suffer the little children to come unto me and forbid them not, for such is the kingdom of heaven ..."

(Matthew 19:14)

Our story begins as many good stories do:

Long ago and far, far away ...

Chapter 1

The Beach

The sun was still shining brightly – as if the day did not want to yield her place. But night was coming soon to claim his portion. A balmy breeze teased the early evening air, providing some relief and attempting to chase away the day's residual heat. Noise from the waves breaking upon the rock-strewn shore intermingled with that of the seagulls calling to one another. Sand was warm between little toes, and closer to the water's edge, it was pretty squishy, too. Laughter from small children rose above the sounds of the beach as they ran and played. Their giggles wafted up, drifting like incense, and were carried away on the gentle wind.

"Those that are pure of heart shall be blessed ..." intoned the young prophet. In appearance, he was an unremarkable man, neither handsome nor ugly. Not especially tall or short, slim or stout – just an average man. He did seem rather young, however, for one so wise. He spoke as if he knew the secrets of life, instead of like one who was seeking to obtain them. Adults stood nearby, parents to the young children, and gravitated toward the young prophet. They gathered around him, mesmerized by his speech and his message of hope.

The children were drawn to him, too. They ran around the adult group, encircling them and laughing. Their run soon slowed, then, halted altogether as they tightened their ring. Closer. Closer they drew, extending their necks, stressing their ears until they could hear the words of the prophet more clearly. His voice was so soothing, his pull was irresistible. Some of the children ventured to peek between the legs of the adults. One bold toddler reached his hand through a gap, his chubby arm stretched to its limit as he strained to reach the prophet.

"No! Misha-el!" His arm was instantly seized by his father, who swung him up and was about to carry him away. The other children saw their opportunity and swarmed through the opening. They tumbled right into the prophet and nearly knocked him over. Horrified at the turn of events, adult hands reached out, grabbing various children. Which child belonged to whom really didn't matter as they sorted through the mayhem. The parents attempted to regain control of the situation, untangling prepubescent limbs as they went. The children squirmed and wriggled deeper into the pile, enjoying their game. They scrambled to avoid the grasping arms of their frantic parents and ran back to the prophet as soon as they found themselves free. The adults were becoming increasingly frustrated at the high jinks of the children.

The man was a prophet, for goodness sake, one parent thought as he dealt with the children's antics. Another parent fumed in embarrassment, "The prophet has no time for such foolishness!" And yet another, formed the thought, *they are bothering him with their childish games.* Also, it was very undignified. No matter the way in which they worded these objections (silently or otherwise), in this, they were all in agreement: the prophet would think their children were unruly if they weren't able to control them. But he merely laughed at their interruption.

"Let them be!" The gentle rebuke of the prophet rang out, his tone full of joy. The adults froze in the midst of retrieving their children. Said children promptly ceased their recalcitrant behavior. The prophet reached for one free child, a little girl, and picked her up. He caressed her hair, spoke softly to her and tucked one finger into her stomach. She giggled and clung to him all the more. He urged the adults again, making welcoming gestures with hands that beckoned.

"Let the little ones come." The parents cautiously released more children at the prophet's insistence. Several onlookers hesitantly brought more children forward when they saw that the prophet received them with gladness.

The young prophet reached out his arms and hugged the children as a group, as many as could fit in his embrace. When there was room for no more, the others crowded in under his arms and returned his hug, giving the effect of a mother hen gathering her baby chicks. The children pressed in close to him, close as they could get, gazing up at the prophet's face. His smile was like the warmth of the sun touching their heads, and it was clear to them, at least, that he loved them immeasurably. Pronouncing a blessing upon the children, he sent them on their way.

Obediently, as if they had never been author and focus of the disturbance, the little ones turned to leave altogether while the adults breathed a collective sigh of relief. The parents made shooing sounds and waving motions with their hands to chase the children off, who ran back to their games, laughing and playing along the shore. Misha-el, whose own father had held him fast during all the fuss, squirmed in his father's arms until he, too, was put down. He toddled over to the prophet to get his own hug and added a soggy kiss. After receiving his own in return, he followed the others to play.

"The heart of a child," the prophet concluded, gesturing at the retreating figure of little Misha-el, "*that* is what you must have to enter the kingdom." The young prophet, the adults mused, always found a way to tie his teachings to this mysterious "kingdom." All roads appeared to lead and end there. Was it his kingdom or his father's? Was it for the future or for right now? Was it to restore their own, now defunct, kingdom? All this talk of a kingdom raised more questions than it answered. But the adults nodded their heads in response, even though they didn't truly understand.

Meanwhile, three older children stood some way off, watching the spectacle. Malachi, being almost a man (he liked to think) was very full of himself.

Hadn't his own father named him man of the house in his absence? The memory made his chest swell with pride. He agreed with the adult thinking that it was quite unseemly to overwhelm the prophet in such a manner. His cousin, Martha, stood also with him. Being of a practical mind herself, she decided that the children would be children. Besides, they were so very young, (babies, even) unlike herself. How could they be expected to restrain themselves?

Another boy, Aristophanes, stood even further off. He wrapped thin arms about himself, hugging his body, suggesting that he was cold when it was actually quite warm. The expressions that ran across his face laid bare his thoughts – first, a sneer, scornful at the children's play – then wistful because he wasn't included. He wasn't really expected to socialize with the other children, he reasoned. After all, his father was not of their culture. Which was why he didn't have any friends, he thought. *And*, because he was new to the area, he liked to add, by way of excuse. He had lots of them – excuses, that is. Aristophanes looked longingly at the group of children, wishing that he could be like them, play like them.

Just at that moment, Ari (for that is what Aristophanes was called) visualized the thought in his mind. The young prophet looked up, over the chaos of the departing children and met his eyes.

"I see we missed a few," he said softly and beckoned to Ari. "You two, too!" the prophet said to Malachi and Martha, smiling at his own pun. Hesitantly, conscious of the many eyes that were suddenly upon them, they walked forward. They needn't have worried about any attention they might have drawn, for at that moment, it seemed all of the adults had something else to do and somewhere else to be. They began to wander off, their minds consumed with some task that demanded their immediate consideration, *right that very minute.*

"*Bo*," the prophet encouraged, motioning with his hand for them to come forward as the space cleared about him. *Come*, he had said in their native tongue, although he had spoken to the adults in the common language. "*Qa-rav*," he urged. *Come near*. More than a little puzzled at how the space about them had cleared so quickly, they obediently complied, albeit haltingly. He smiled at their dubious approach. "Don't dawdle so. Let me look upon you." When they stood before him, he looked at them solemnly but at the same time, with a twinkle in his eye. He had kind eyes as if he liked to laugh. He looked them over and walked around them, sizing them up.

With his naturally brown skin made even more so by time spent in the sun, Malachi was still a boy but big for his age. He was already broad of shoulder and sturdy. Stout is how his mom normally referred to his stature. Most other folks just called him *gadol*, or big, like his father. Thick brow, broad nose, wide mouth –

even his facial features seemed larger than average. Maybe he'd be even bigger than his father one day.

Ari shrank back under the prophet's scrutiny. He was lanky, slighter of frame than Mal but no less sturdy from helping his uncles carry their tent making materials. His features broadcast his mixed heritage – hair blond but tightly curled, with grey eyes and a profile made up of sharp angles that looked as if it had been sculpted from stone. He shuffled and shifted on his feet under the steady gaze of the prophet. *Stop fidgeting*; he could hear his mom say. He willed his limbs to be still.

Last of all stood Martha, with her small, delicate features. She had very beautiful hair and eyes so dark brown they actually appeared to be black. Martha was "on the cusp of beauty," as her mom often told her. But she just didn't see it. She hoped one day that she would grow to be as lovely as her oldest sister, Fatima, who was the mirror image of their mother. It was a faint hope, Martha knew, for she had inherited a smaller version (only slightly, it seemed) of her father's nose. Her hand crept up to hide the offending protuberance from the prophet's inspection.

"Hmmm," the prophet murmured, almost to himself. He narrowed his eyes as if trying to see far away. "Yes," he nodded his head, in confirmation to his own inner conversation and touched his fingertip to his pursed lips, tapping lightly. He looked pleased and concluded: "These will do."

"What to do, how to do?" he speculated aloud but still, to himself. He lifted his hands and looked back and forth, at one hand then the other. The children exchanged glances and scrunched their faces up at him, wondering what he was doing. "Let's see. Two hands, three heads – how should we handle this?" The question must have been rhetorical for he continued on, an indication that he didn't expect an answer. In any case, the children surely had no answer because they didn't know what he was trying to do. The prophet rested his left hand on Malachi's shoulder and repositioned him in the middle of the two smaller children. Looking at Ari, then Martha, he drew them forward on each side and placed his hands upon their heads. "You'll have to help me with this part. I need you to hold hands."

A little uncertain about what was supposed to be happening, they gave each other sideways glances and reached out for Malachi's hands. Immediately, they felt a warm, prickly sensation (kind of like all over goose bumps) which traveled from head to toe, then back up and through their arms and out through their fingertips, from Martha, from Ari and into Mal.

Then, the prophet turned his face skyward and spoke words over them – wonderful words in a different language. Words full of power that they shouldn't be able to understand but somehow, they did. *Blessed. Called. Ordained.* **Chosen!** At the last word, his voice echoed in crescendo, breaking over them. Loud, booming, and yet, not – his words rang out and resonated within Mal, Ari and Martha to the depths of their beings. His voice ricocheted about and filled all the spaces of their minds. To the dark recesses, it brought illumination. It consumed, but did not. The atmosphere surrounding them grew so thick and heavy that his words became nearly tangible. They hung suspended in the air as if on strings, and the early evening sky seemed to shimmer about them. As the words faded, their world tilted and went black.

Chapter 2

Ari

… opened his eyes. He was in his own bedroom, if you could call it that. It was really more of a designated sleeping area in his home. His cloak, which lay over him, functioned as pillow, cover or bedding as needed. Mantle, he mentally corrected himself. His outer garment was known as a cloak where he came from, but around here, it was more often called a mantle. But it was a nice cloak, nicer than some, and a carryover from a time when things were much better for his family. His tunic was of good quality, too. His fine clothing didn't quite fit in properly with his surroundings, he knew. And he still couldn't get used to this new, *poor* way of living.

Not too long ago, they'd lived in a fine home. At the time, Ari had a real bed. His father was a Roman centurion, one of their best and most fearless fighters and a respected leader among them. When he'd unexpectedly died, Ari's mom decided to move back to her childhood home, in this small fishing village, to be near her family. His heart squeezed tight in his chest at the thought of his *patér*, the memory of his death still too fresh. Ari missed him so but tried not to mention it too much. Not a day went by that he didn't think of him. Being of an easygoing nature, he had resolved to stay strong for his mom and so, tried to put on a good face.

He knew things couldn't be good for her either. His mom came to live with her family so that she could get the help she needed to raise her son. Being home also made her feel better. Family eased the pain of their loss and helped them both to heal. This home was humble, but it was the best his grandfather could do. Not that Ari was ungrateful. Without family, they would be in desperate straits, indeed. He sighed, inwardly. It still took some getting used to.

Images from his sleep still danced in his head. Ari rubbed his face and shook his head to clear the cobwebs. That didn't help. The last thing he remembered was the beach and that man, the prophet, "praying" for him. His memory was a bit vague. But was it a dream? He'd just lifted himself to rest on his elbows when his mother walked in.

"Mama?" He was about to question her about what happened when she broke in:

"Good morning, my lamb!" she said, cheerily when she saw that he'd awakened.

"Mom!" Ari's eyebrows furrowed and he looked around quickly to see if anyone was around to overhear the childhood moniker. He didn't want *that* made public. He mainly objected to her pet name for him because it was so babyish. He wasn't a lamb. He was a man! Well, almost. But to her, he would always be her little *seh*. Argh, he groaned mentally but otherwise, made no more outcries against his mom's habit. He left her the familiar practice as a small comfort of a happier time.

"It's about time you rose. You fell asleep on the beach! We couldn't rouse you. The Young Master said you were tired, you and the other children, and that we should just let you rest. Your uncle carried you all the way home. You didn't stir the entire time!" On and on she chattered, but the rest was lost on Ari. She'd answered his question.

So *that's* how he got home. It wasn't a dream. Maybe all of it really did happen. But how much of it was real? So many questions bounced around in his head. He was curious but decided to leave the solving of that mystery for later. The details were still too fuzzy for him to make sense of anything.

Ari rose from his bed, thinking that some cool water would refresh him and help sort things out. He strapped on his sandals, with the intent of heading outside to draw water from the well. His mom must have been thinking along those same lines, for she handed him a clay pitcher on his way out. He looked at her and raised one eyebrow to perfection. She did it right back, crossing her arms and looking smug. Mama had taught him that very move. Ari grinned, took the pitcher from her hand and headed out the doorway.

It wasn't normally cold during this time of year, but mornings could be chilly. The day was just dawning, and it promised to be sunny. Ari knew the sun would soon drive away the frigid temperature. Shivering, he hurried to draw the water so he could get back inside where it was nice and warm.

The well was more of a cistern, actually. The true well was community property and set in the heart of the village, amongst an odd assortment of houses. In Ari's opinion, the homes looked skewed with their random angles and heights, chosen according to the whims and financial standing of the owners. His grandfather's home, it seemed to Ari, was more uniform, well planned and pleasing to the eye. Then again, he could be biased.

The family's *bor* was located in the courtyard of his grandfather's home and created to catch rainwater. Its lid was level with the ground, and a rope hung from a wooden wheel which sat over the well. The mouth of the cistern was fortified with rocks, imbedded in a circle around the opening. Ari heaved the stone lid aside and began to use the rope to draw the vessel up so that he could pour the water into his waiting pitcher.

The *tey-vah* wasn't a proper container, really. Being made of animal skin, it was quite flimsy and somewhat floppy. The water sloshed over the sides as it flexed and strained under the weight of the load. Ari hurried to draw the water, his movements a bit jerky because his fingers were getting cold. The morning seemed especially frigid; he just knew the water would be even more so. Finally, the container, brimming full with water, reached the top of the well. Ari quickly reached for it, but in his haste, he caused the container to buckle and the freezing water spilled over the sides.

Ari jumped back to avoid the splash of cold water and heaved up more in the process. His hands froze in midair, and he tried to hold the collapsing water skin away from himself. A cry escaped his lips as he shut his eyes, averted his head and braced himself. He knew he would be drenched in the freezing water. He heard the sloshing of water and held his breath, waiting for the shock of icy liquid to soak his skin. Then … nothing. No cold, damp feeling to his clothes. Bewildered, he slowly peeled open one eye, then the other.

The water pooled on the ground near his feet, yet he was bone dry. He let out the breath he had been holding. He was relieved, but couldn't fathom how he'd been able to avoid getting doused. Ari leaned in to look closer. The water formed a semi-circle like a crescent moon, glistening weirdly, just out of reach of his toes. He peered down at the strangeness of it and stepped closer. The puddle of water *moved*.

Chapter 3

Martha

... didn't question how she wound up on her tiny pallet in her home. Because she was so small, she was kind of used to people picking her up and carting her around like a sack of grain. Martha didn't mind, really – it came in handy when she was tired. As she must have been last night, she thought.

Quite sensibly, she reasoned, she must have fallen asleep on the beach and dreamed the events of the day before. She further deduced that she must have slept for a long time – the remainder of the day and into the night, but she couldn't remember what she could have possibly done to warrant such exhaustion. Maybe she was coming down with something, she surmised.

She rose from her pallet, cooed at her baby sister lying in the hammock and grabbed a quick breakfast. Mother must be nearby, she knew. She tore off a piece of *le-hhem*, pairing the flatbread with goat cheese and a handful of grapes. She ate quickly while she stood, before beginning her morning chores. It was quite late, she now realized. The older children usually rose at dawn to carry out their duties, caring for livestock and the like, while Martha stayed home and helped her mother with housework and cooking. But her siblings were long gone. Mother must have allowed her to sleep in this morning. Maybe she thought Martha was sick, too.

It had grown cold during the night, Martha could feel it. She was glad for the warmth provided by the remains of the small fire left in the pit in the center of their home. Dying coals burned cheerily in the brazier, and she imagined her mother must have cooked there this morning. What she couldn't understand was how she had slept through all the preparations and her family eating breakfast. Usually, they caused enough of a disturbance to wake even the soundest sleeper.

Feeling guilty because Mother had prepared breakfast alone and cleaned up afterwards, she decided she could puzzle it out while going about her chores. One of her responsibilities was to sweep and tidy their living space. Martha spied the broom made of branches in the corner. Sunlight streamed in patches through the lattice work of a nearby window, further evidence of her dereliction of duties.

Sighing, she fetched the broom and went to work on the hard, packed dirt. She smoothed the earthen floor as she went, sweeping the area around the fire's pit carefully, or so she thought. But the next thing she knew her broom was on fire! Not just any fire but a tall column of fire, nearly reaching the ceiling. It *whooshed* up in front of her with a great leap. Martha screamed, dropped the broom and leaped out of harm's way.

Martha threw her hands out to protect herself, but at her scream, the column of fire froze in midair. As she watched in astonishment, the column began to revolve slowly. Then the fire was swallowed up and replaced by smoke? No – a cloud; a smoky, cloudy pillar where, only moments before, there had been a shaft of fire. The swirling cylinder of smoke reversed direction. Martha's mouth gaped open.

"Martha, what are you doing?"

"Huh?" Martha spun on her heel at her mother's voice, then whirled back around to look at the pillar so quickly that it almost made her dizzy. It was gone. Did it disappear? Collapse? She couldn't tell. Martha looked down at the broom. It wasn't even singed. She couldn't smell the smoke, either. She looked at the glowing embers of the fire pit. They seemed the very picture of normal; smoldering sleepily as if they had never wakened.

"You screamed," Mother prodded. "Is there something wrong?"

Thinking herself to be more ill than she'd initially believed, and maybe just a bit feverish, Martha replied: "Oh, THAT. *Er*. Yes ..." Her voice trailed off in confusion. How could she explain what she saw? *Delirium*, she mentally diagnosed. The back of her hand went to her forehead. She had imagined the fire. Maybe.

In the end, she went with the most plausible explanation. "I just ... *thought* I saw something ... but I – I," she stammered, "I must have imagined it," she finished, quickly. She was seeing things. That was the only logical conclusion.

"Gahhhh!" The baby clapped and pointed at the broom. She made clucking and smacking noises with her mouth. Martha's eyes widened, and she translated: *she saw it, too?*

"Hmmm," said Mother, giving her daughter a keen look, "well, if you're feeling better, you can get on with your cleaning." She touched Martha's forehead and checked her temperature before adding, "And, I'll need your help with the cooking, soon. I'm expecting company."

"Yes, Mother," Martha answered, in a distracted sort of way. She looked at the broom, warily. Mother came and stood over her, looking down at the broom, too.

"It won't be picking itself up, dear," Mother gently coaxed.

"Oh! Right!" Martha tentatively picked up the broom and slowly, cautiously began to sweep, again.

****

Darkness.

Everywhere, darkness.

The creature stirred, slithering in the eternal night.

Awareness came to him. A flicker of recognition.

An awakening of a gift … a power? No, a weapon.

Not again. Not this time.

He would not be beaten.

Chapter 4

Mal

… awakened to a touch on his arms. None too gentle, little fingers on chubby hands were attached to his arm, pushing and pulling alternately, urgently. He cracked open an eyelid.

"Mal, WAKE UP!" A childish voice insisted.

"Uhm up, uhm up," Mal mumbled and groaned, turning over on his side. He nestled his head into his folded arms as he sought a more comfortable position. *Thump!* The sound near his head startled him into wakefulness. He felt groggy. He opened his eyes further, now more awake, though not yet fully functional. Hannah, his little sister, stood before him with her hands on her hips and looking very mother-*ish*. He supposed that made sense because she'd seen their mother assume that pose too many times.

"Ma-al!" Hannah was feeling especially aggravated by him, so she stretched his name out over two syllables. She stomped her foot, again, to get his attention and a little more respect since he was ignoring her summons. "Mama said to tell you, 'Get up, lazy bones! The morning is far spent!'"

Hannah's bare feet were in his line of vision, and he couldn't help but notice the level of grime upon them. The sun had barely risen, and her feet were already caked. How was that possible? But that was Hannah for you. She had always been an early riser, even as an infant. She was usually up in plenty of time to get dirty; doing whatever it was she did to get so dirty. Mal waited, knowing what was coming next – Hannah was so predictable.

Sure enough, she extended her right leg and nudged him with a grubby foot, which he promptly grabbed and pulled her off balance. She held onto the wall and hopped on one leg as she fought to stay upright. Shrieking and giggling, she watched as his other hand moved towards the outstretched foot he held captive.

"No, Mal! No!" Hannah laughed and screamed. She gave up all efforts to remain standing and fell on her bottom, trying to scoot away and make her escape. But Mal still held her foot prisoner. He made exaggerated tickling motions with his fingers and wagged his eyebrows up and down, playing the part of the dastardly villain while Hannah squealed and tried to pull her foot away. He stopped his fingers in midair, just before touching her foot. It was time to negotiate.

"If I let you go, will you give me a few more minutes?" He bargained with Hannah all the time. It was what they did. She could be relentless, but she always folded when he threatened to tickle her, although he never did – much.

"Mal's up," he heard a voice say – likely, his sister, Abby. Giving up the game and Hannah's foot,

Mal blew out a breath and reached for Hannah's hand. He pretended to allow her to help him up.

Mal struggled to his feet and leaned some of his weight on Hannah. Not too much, but just enough so that she could feel as though she was helping. Hannah liked to be useful. He groaned loudly as he went, feigning a limp for full effect. Hannah valiantly escorted him to the low table for breakfast.

"See how strong you are, Hannah? I couldn't have done it without you," Mal said. Hannah waited until he took his seat on the mat, before replying.

"See, Mama? I woke him up!" she announced jubilantly.

"Yes, you did, my precious! I knew you could do it," Mama replied. She was a large, big boned woman that somehow matched her husband perfectly. She leaned over and kissed the top of Hannah's head, then added extra encouragement, "You're such a big help to your *eym*!" Hannah beamed at the praise, her duty to Mama fulfilled. Mama rubbed Hannah's arms briskly and then ruffled Mal's hair, by way of good morning. She paused to whisper into his ear, "Stop teasing your *a-hhot*." But she wasn't upset, not truly, and kissed the top of his head to show him.

It went like this most mornings. Mal's mom thought it was cute to send his baby sister to wake him ('cause, sometimes only she could wake him). It had become a bit of a morning ritual. They knew Hannah had been successful when they heard the shrieks and giggles emanating as Mal threatened to tickle her. Hannah's persistence usually paid off. It worked like a charm every time. *Even last night*, he thought, remembering suddenly.

She had awakened him at the beach. Mal recalled dragging himself to his feet, at her insistence, and stumbling most of the way home. *Almost like sleepwalking.* Though he'd be hard pressed to call it sleep, as Hannah complained all the way when he didn't carry her. He couldn't. He was so exhausted that when he got home, all he could do was crawl into bed where he fell into a deep sleep.

He felt better this morning. Much more alert. His mother looked pointedly over her shoulder and nodded at the diminished wood pile. Mal took the hint. He stood, preparing to go outside and gather more wood for the cooking fire so his mom could finish getting breakfast ready. As soon as he announced his intention, Hannah looked up at him mournfully, her bottom lip pouty.

"Can I come, too?" she asked, looking woebegone. Mal paused with his hand on the door. He didn't need to turn and look at her to get the full visual effect. He knew Hannah was doing her best impression of a sad puppy. It was the face she always put on when she wanted to get her way. Hannah was used to being indulged. Being cute went a long way. His mother cleared her throat, but Mal didn't look her way. He knew just what her eyes would say: *Take your sister with you!*

"Come on!" Mal rolled his eyes and grumbled good-naturedly. He sighed loudly as he opened the door and gestured outside. He really didn't mind her coming with him, but he had to put on a token show of resistance so she would feel as though she'd overcome his objections. It worked. Hannah promptly leapt up and skipped out the door ahead of him before he could change his mind.

"You fell for the ol' puppy face!" Hannah sang as she went past him, her forlorn expression forgotten in her triumph.

"Spoiled!" Mal called after her and shut the door behind them. She was.

Chapter 5

Mal loved being outdoors. He went down the well-worn path, heading toward an awning of trees. Hannah knew the way well and skipped ahead. Collecting firewood was normally a simple process and fairly easy. Usually, after a storm or a bout of high winds, tree limbs could be found strewn along the ground haphazardly. Hannah collected small twigs, branches and pieces of bark while Mal collected and carried larger pieces.

With Hannah on hand, the task would also become more time consuming. She made a game out of it and pointed to larger limbs (for him to carry) that she thought would fit "perfectly" in their fire place. She would be responsible for the smaller pieces that were fed to mother's cooking stove. She took the duty seriously, giving the impression she was measuring the pieces by seeing them there in her mind. He shook his head at the thought. Hannah could become so attached to things; he wouldn't be surprised if she wanted to name her twigs.

Mal watched as she picked out choice pieces of wood and obediently added them to his bundle. He tried to keep a straight face as Hannah did her very best to imitate their mom, ordering him around as though she were in charge. Mal found it easier to hold back his laughter when he reminded himself that he was doing a bit of imitating, too. He was doing his level best to act mature and responsible.

Their father, a fisherman, was often away from their family for long periods of time. Mal was left in charge to protect and provide for his mom and younger sisters in his father's place. Mal took this charge seriously and indulged his little sister as his father would because he knew how much she (and they all) missed their father. In quick fashion, they'd gathered plenty of firewood and Mal turned to leave with his arms full.

"Come on, Hannah!" Mal called as he went, "Let's go!"

Just then, he heard a loud, ominous, creaking sound behind him. It came from over his head – in Hannah's direction. He turned back to look and halted. Time seemed to slow down so that he could capture the full horror of their predicament. Hannah had heard the noise, too. Her face was turned upward, her mouth opened in a silent scream. He followed her gaze and saw the huge limb break away from the trunk of the tree and fall. Mal feared it was big enough to break poor Hannah at the speed it was falling.

He dropped the bundle of wood and dashed towards his little sister, desperate to remove her from the tree limb's path. He was too far away! He wasn't going to make it in time. Panicked, he screamed her name and lunged forward. The wind seemed to catch him and carry him forward as he stretched his entire body out, throwing his arms out to save her. Mal hit the ground with a thud but didn't pause long enough

45

to register pain. His arms scrambled crazily, reaching out for Hannah. He grabbed her to him and wrapped himself protectively around her. He shielded her body with his own as she put her hands over her own head and curled into a ball under him.

Breathing heavily, they lay like that for a few moments, bracing themselves for the blow that never came. As the realization seeped in, Mal opened his eyes and lifted his head. Wondrously, the huge tree limb lay on the ground a few feet from them. He was so caught up in protecting her from harm that he hadn't heard it land. Puzzled but grateful, Mal offered up a silent prayer of thanks and unfurled himself from around Hannah, who was pretty shaken up. She was sobbing and crying hysterically but still clutching her treasured twigs to her chest.

"You're fine, Hannah!" Mal attempted to calm her down as he helped her up. "We're both fine, see?" He made a great show of brushing off her clothes and keeping up a steady stream of chatter to distract her.

"It's – we are well, truly!" he insisted. "Not a scratch on us! And you were brave, too!"

"I-I w-was?" Hannah's stammering sobs subsided. She began to do that hiccupping thing that people do when they're trying to stop crying.

"Yes! Yes! You were *so* brave. You didn't even scream." Mal thought it best not to mention that she had likely been too paralyzed with fear. "You only cried just a little bit," he demonstrated by squeezing his thumb and index finger together, leaving a small space, "at the very end. That was very, very brave of you." He nodded slowly, punctuating each "very" with his head movement for extra emphasis.

"I was brave?" The waterworks halted, just for a moment. She looked up at her big brother with huge eyes from a tear streaked face. "I was bra-have!" She hiccupped again, and her bottom lip quivered. She struggled, manfully, to keep it together. She did want to be a big girl for her brother. She sniffed. That was all it took. Her face crumpled, and the floodgates opened as she gave in. It was all more than poor Hannah could take.

Mal picked her up and hauled her over his shoulder while she bawled, knowing it was useless. Only their mom could calm her down now. He grabbed a few pieces of the fallen wood and left the bulk to come back and collect later. Now that the danger had passed, he began to think and replay the events in his mind. Was it his imagination, or did the wind propel him forward and help him to save Hannah? He looked back to the huge limb and to Hannah, safe in his arms. Whatever the cause, he was thankful. He looked to the heavens and mouthed a prayer of gratitude for his and Hannah's safety.

"I was bra-ha-have!" Hannah continued to hiccup and sob repeatedly as he carried her home.

"Yes, you were," Mal said between intervals, patting her back and consoling his distraught younger sibling.

Among the shadows cast by the trees, one emerged, separated and watched as Mal carried his crying sister down the path.

Chapter 6

Strange things, indeed …

He'd watched an egg roll off a table once – maybe the table or the floor was crooked. He didn't know which. Either way, his mom was pretty miffed that he'd watched the egg roll off the table and crash onto the floor. As then, he wondered if perhaps he was standing on an incline. But, no, the ground about him appeared to be level enough.

As Ari stood near the lip of the open well, he imagined he was "playing" with the puddle of water – as if it were sentient. He repeated the game several times, just to be certain. Yes. The water seemed to be *avoiding* his feet. As he stepped forward, the puddle moved forward, always just out of reach of his toes.

"Huh?" The sound startled him until he realized it had come from him. He scratched his head.

Then he rubbed his face. He ran the palm of his hand along his jawline, across his mouth and down his neck as he tried to make sense of it. His hand came to rest on his chest, rubbing distractedly, and he was still no closer to an answer.

For good measure, Ari chased the puddle of water around the well, trying to step into the water. Same result. His feet remained dry. He attempted to analyze the situation, once more. Just what was going on here? Water didn't just move of its own volition. Did it? And although, at times, his mother may have accused him of having an aversion to water, it had never avoided him. No – he reassured himself. Otherwise, how could he have taken a bath?

"No," he said aloud to himself, again.   Oh! Now, he was talking to himself. Folks would surely think him mad if he was overheard, and he wouldn't blame them. He was starting to doubt his own sanity in this. First, moving puddles and then, talking to himself. Could he get any crazier?

"I wish you would just go away!" he hissed at the puddle, for it was evidence of his lunacy. The puddle slithered obediently to the opening of the well and slid quietly back in. Ari's eyes widened at the sight. That was beyond strange.

"And water that moves on my command," Ari muttered in disbelief. He rolled his eyes, thinking his sanity had just slipped over the edge along with the puddle of water. "I may as well talk to myself since I really am going crazy."

"Ari!" His mom called. "What is taking so long?"

Ari jumped at the sound of her voice. He was so preoccupied that he had forgotten about his pitcher, which now lay overturned on the ground. Oh, how to explain this? He couldn't, other than the obvious "INSANE" title he'd recently acquired. *Be sure to add nervous and jumpy to the list*, his inner voice prodded.

"Oh, be quiet," he said to his inner crazy. To his mom, he called, "Coming!" He picked up the well container, peered into it anxiously and wondered if there were any more of that "special" water inside. But it lay calm and serene now; there was no suspicious movement. It looked normal. Safe.

"Ari!" his mom called again, sounding more impatient, which ended his internal debate. Settling on the more feasible and acceptable explanation – the water was fine; therefore, he was a lunatic – he carefully filled his pitcher with water and dropped the container back into the well. It hit the water with a satisfying and, rather ordinary, splash. No sign of his weird water puddle friend either. See? He told himself. Safe.

Ari replaced the stone lid on the well, picked up his pitcher of water and turned to go home. Just then, a thought suddenly occurred to him: What if he wasn't crazy? He thought of his encounter with that prophet, the Young Master, all but forgotten during this morning's antics. What if something about him had changed?

Knowing it sounded insane – *add it to the list, buddy*, his inner voice chided – he realized last night wasn't a dream. Maybe the water wasn't special. Maybe *he* was special. Ari needed answers, and he knew just where to begin. He had to see the Young Master again. He hurriedly finished his chores, packed a few snacks and braved the heat of the midday sun to seek answers for the bizarre happenings.

Chapter 7

The Beach, again …

It was well after midday when they saw him once more. The day had grown as warm as it promised to be earlier, and the sun shone brilliantly even as it receded. Most people normally rested during this time. They sat out the hottest part of the day, seeking refuge from the sweltering heat. Not Ari, Mal and Martha. The three children could not rest. They seemed to be drawn there of one accord. And there he was – the Young Master. They watched as he stooped and drew lines in the sand with his finger, seeming not to notice them.

The children unconsciously assumed identical positions as the day before, each one mimicking their previous stances, a little way off from the prophet. Mal saw Ari and nodded at him. Ari returned the nod, a little surprised to see Mal there, too. He was a little more than shocked that Mal actually acknowledged him. Most of the kids his own age acted like he wasn't there, so he treated them with a similar lack of regard. Normally, he responded to them by lifting his chin a little higher and looking down his nose at them. As though he were above it all; as though he were better than them. That move hadn't won him any friends.

Martha was there, too, he'd noticed. But why? He knew his own reason for coming. He had a special problem, which he thought may have been a direct result of the events of yesterday. Could it be that they all had the same problem? Not wanting to reveal his own inner turmoil but compelled by curiosity, he opened his mouth to speak.

"Did you ...?" The three voices spoke as one. Obviously, the compulsion had overtaken them all at the same time. Initially, their expressions were puzzled, and then cleared as it dawned on them: Maybe they all had a special problem! They came together quickly, talking excitedly, in hushed voices.

They didn't want to be overheard, although the beach was strangely deserted. They snuck sideways glances at the Young Master, who now sat in the same spot as yesterday, continuing to write in the sand with his finger.

"What happened to you?" They chorused altogether and tried again. Mal placed his hand on his chest and began.

"I could have sworn the wind helped me today! I think it blew a huge tree limb away and saved my little sister!" He gestured with his hands wildly, creating a picture without more words.

"My broom was on fire! And then it wasn't!" Martha spoke in a rush, her words tumbling over one another. She took a breath and forced herself to calm down and speak more slowly. "I thought I had a fever, but then I remembered what happened last night and so I came back here. I don't know what I expected to find. I just *hoped* …" Martha's voice trailed off and she hid her face in her hands. "I don't know what I hoped to find – I just knew I had to come here."

"Um, I played with a puddle of water today?" said Ari, lamely. There didn't seem to be much point in saying more than that. It would be just like adding more to the crazy. In unison, the children huddled together and turned their attention to the prophet.

Just at that moment, the Young Master stopped writing and looked up at them. "Well – I suppose you could ask me," the prophet offered. "If you are quite finished, that is."

Chapter 8

Answers …

Mal, Ari and Martha stepped forward, woodenly – again, in echo of their movements yesterday. This time, though, they were not concerned with prying eyes that wanted to see all. There was only one set of eyes that mattered, and they seemed to know all. At least, all that the children wanted to know. They stopped at the outer edge of a circle he had drawn in the sand, which contained strange writings, symbols and words they'd never seen before. Fidgeting again, Ari shuffled from one foot to the other as he met the Young Master's piercing gaze.

"So, I gathered you'd like to know what all of this is about. Yes?" He crouched on the ground before them, one knee in the sand, still within his circle. The children, who had previously been quite talkative, were now shy and reserved. Suddenly reluctant to verbalize their thoughts, they looked at him with wide eyes, which asked the question for them: what had been done to them? Ari cast his eyes down and scuffed his foot in the sand.

"You three have been given very special gifts for a very special purpose, should you choose to accept. You may use your gifts, as you will, whenever you feel the time is right. I trust your judgment; I believe you will use these gifts to serve, which is why you have been called."

"Why us?" Ari interrupted the Young Master's monologue, emboldened by his curiosity.

"Yes, why choose me?" said Mal, his tongue loosened, too.

"Or me," blurted Martha, not to be outdone.

"What is your name?" The Young Master held up his hand to halt their inquiries. He turned to face Ari first, answering his question with a question.

"Aristophanes – Ari for short," he responded, wondering what that had to do with anything. His mom was always on him for answering her question with a question of his own.

"Ari is the name your father gave you – what is the name of your mother's people?" The prophet persisted.

Ari hesitated. How did the prophet know about his little used name? No one had called him that in forever. Most people chose to call him by the name of his father's culture. He was never allowed to forget that he was different.

"I am also called Mika`el," Ari replied. "That's the name I was given by my mother when I was born."

The Young Master stood and straightened. He looked up and to the side as if he were thinking about how much to reveal or how much he should say. Then he grasped Ari's arms firmly and hunched over him so that they were at eye level. Looking at him gravely, he said, "It is not a name to be taken lightly. It's a very special name, chosen by your mother with great care; it is the name of a great warrior and prince. And I expect, one day, you will live up to your namesake." Ari swallowed and raised his eyebrow at that revelation. That was a lot to take in. He felt the weight of his name fall on him.

"And you, young Malachi." The Young Master straightened and turned to Mal. Mal jumped at the sound of his name, for he didn't recall giving it to the prophet. The Young Master placed his hand on Mal's shoulder as he continued, "You were named for a great prophet and messenger of God. And so you shall be." He met Mal's eyes and squeezed his shoulder, encouragingly.

"Martha." He touched her cheek gently and cupped her chin, lifting her face up towards him. He bent his head down to meet her gaze. "You touch my heart so. You remind me of another very practical Martha that I know. Sometimes practical is good. We all need to be reminded to take care of things that are necessary. But sometimes necessary and practical do not coincide. Understand?"

She nodded her head vigorously, suggesting she did, but in truth, she had no idea what he was talking about. What he said wasn't logical or practical. In fact, it was a bit confusing. But she didn't like to ask. She could be pretty resourceful, when put to it. She had lots of answers to things, many of which were gleaned by sitting in the company of adults. She nodded anyway, in the hopes that she might figure it out later.

"No, you don't understand now," the prophet wasn't fooled. "But one day, you shall."

"What do our names have to do with any of this?" Ari broke in, again. He just didn't see the connection.

"Ah! But it is more than just your names." The prophet turned to face Ari, again. "It's also your character that I'm looking at. I've known you for –" he broke off, catching himself and did that upward, sideways thing with his eyes again. "Let's just say, I've known you and watched you for a while. You see, you've come to a point in your lives when choices will soon become very important to you. The decisions you make now can impact the rest of your lives, so you must make good choices."

He paused here, and steepled his fingers, making a triangle of his forefingers and thumbs. Another internal debate traveled across his face. When he spoke again, he seemed to choose his words deliberately and, with great care.

"You may meet some people during your mission who are also about to make some important, life changing decisions themselves. My hope is that you can help them and yourselves at the same time. Your journey is the same. Therefore, I can use you."

The Young Master stopped abruptly and closed his eyes. A puff of air stirred about him, swirling the sand a bit and lifting strands of hair around his upturned face. The children watched his chest rise and fall as he breathed in, deeply, and then exhaled. He appeared to be listening. The prophet cocked his head to the side and nodded. *Another person speaking to his inner voice*, Ari thought wryly. He came to attention at the sound of his name.

"The choice I set before you today – Ari, Mal, Martha," the Young Master opened his eyes and looked at each of them (especially hard, it seemed, at Ari) in turn before continuing, "is simple and yet, not. It will change your life, but it has to be your decision." He rose to his feet and stepped back, further into his circle on the sand. "It won't be easy. It won't always be fun. Sometimes, it may be even seem dangerous. But it will never be more than you can handle. I have good plans for you. Never forget that! No matter how things may seem. The question is, will you accept?" He made a sweeping gesture with his arm, following the line of the circle.

Each of them considered his question: How could they say yes without knowing what it entailed? Ari squared his shoulders and lifted his chin. He wasn't sure what made him want to cross that line. Maybe it was the thought of being used by the Young Master. For some reason, he realized, the idea truly appealed to him. Cautiously, he stepped into the circle.

Martha wasn't sure why she wanted to cross the line either, maybe because he chose *her*. The Young Master's cryptic comments didn't exactly inspire confidence. There was too much she didn't know. And that last part about "It will never be more than you can handle," left her feeling doubtful. Her Momma always said: *Pray that you will never have to bear all that you are able to endure.* Then again, Martha was used to being the smallest and most insignificant member of her family. And also, the most practical. Inwardly, she sighed. No one ever chose her for anything except housework. Maybe she wanted to be *impractical*, just once. So, despite her misgivings, she stepped into the circle.

Mal would do it because, being almost a man, he felt he could take on the responsibility. Wasn't he used to taking care of his family on his father's behalf? Shouldn't that care also extend to his small cousin Martha? Besides, these two *young ones* (although, in reality, they were not much younger than he) could do with some looking after. He was needed so he would do it, simple as that. He was all about being dependable now, he added. AND, he didn't like being shown up – how was it that Ari got to be the warrior of the group? Perhaps the prophet had gotten them mixed up. That must be the reason. Wanting to prove himself, into the circle he stepped.

In the end, they all stepped into the circle, following each other so closely it almost seemed simultaneous. They looked around guardedly, expecting to fall unconscious again. Nothing happened. Well. That was that.

"You may use your gifts as you will, keeping in mind," the Young Master continued, "that with great gifts come even greater responsibility. Before now, my servant, Moses, was the only human vessel to wield all four talents. Between the three of you, all four exist, once again. Ari, as you have seen, you have been given power over water. It will obey you. Mal – you are in control of wind. It will come to your aid. Together you and Ari have command over the wind and the waves. And Martha," he came to stand in front of her and touched her head, ruffling her hair. "Small Martha, now you are not so insignificant. You shall have two powers. You have been given dominion over fire *and* cloud." Her eyes grew big at that.

"I must go," he announced unexpectedly. He straightened and made motions as if he were dusting sand particles off his hands. He also brushed the grains off his garments, brusquely. "Make good use of your talents. Give it a try and we'll see how it works out." He finished abruptly, nodding in a manner which indicated that was the end of it. He turned and began to walk away as if he had somewhere else to be. The children looked at each other, dumbfounded. Ari rushed forward.

"Wait!" he shouted at the Young Master's retreating figure.

"Yes, Ari?" The prophet halted and answered without turning around.

"Is that all there is?" Ari questioned, almost belligerently. His eyebrows drew together, and his expression balled up. Belatedly, he remembered his manners and caught himself. Powers? Mission? The words rebounded in his head. It was too much to absorb at once.

"Yes, Ari," the prophet responded, patiently.

"Well, I just thought there would be more ..." Ari said, this time more respectfully. He was at a loss for more words and held his hands out towards the prophet's back, beseechingly.

"Yes, Ari?" The prophet turned and sighed. He clasped his hands in front of him. Extra emphasis was put on the *yes*.

"Uhm ... help?" Ari finished, inadequately. It was the only word he could think of.

"Don't worry, Ari – it will come to you all when you need it." His voice faded into the distance as he turned again and walked away until all they could hear was the sound of the waves lapping the shore. The Young Master was gone.

Chapter 9

Lead to more questions ...

"Well, I like him and all but he wasn't much help." Ari joked in the silence. Mal turned to him and glared. This wasn't the time for jests. He was still recovering from the shock of having this "assignment" dropped into their laps. They still knew very little about these *gifts* and what they were supposed to do with them.

Martha sat, or rather flopped down into the sand. Her legs suddenly felt boneless and gave out. This whole ordeal was rather trying and had taken a lot out of her. She didn't even know how much time they had been given. Was there even a time limit on their gifts? Did they lose them if they didn't use them? And how could she make her gift do what it did this morning? There were so many unanswered questions.

Mal stood with his arms folded across his chest, thinking. Somebody had to take the lead and, being the oldest, that somebody should be him. It certainly wasn't going to be Ari, *the warrior*, he snuffed mentally. The thought of that still rankled. Anyway, Mal thought, he had it all figured out. Well, part of it, at least.

"The first thing we want to do is find out how our gifts work," Mal suggested. That seemed as good a place to start as any. "Do I have the strength of the wind? Does it make me stronger?" he queried. He wondered if that were even possible. He was already bigger than everyone his age and hardier, too. Mal flexed his meaty biceps, honed from years of hauling in fishing nets with his father, and slapped his upper arms a few times. He walked over to a large boulder. He tried to lift it, but the rock wouldn't budge. He strained as he pulled, his muscles bulging. "Argh!" he yelled with a great heave. Nothing.

"Guess not," Ari muttered derisively under his breath while Mal walked it off, swinging his arms and trying to ensure he hadn't hurt himself in the process. Ari lifted one eyebrow at Martha and smirked, just a little. She giggled in response, and then quickly sobered. At least Mal was trying to resolve their problem, whatever his methods. When Mal pegged him with a look, Ari hid the sound of his choked laughter behind his hand before straightening his expression. He dropped his hand to his side, with a wide-eyed, innocent look in place.

"I remember being really frightened when I saw the fire. I screamed, and it stopped. Well – it froze. Maybe it comes when we're afraid?" Martha offered helpfully.

"That could make sense." Ari nodded his head in agreement, thinking of his own experience. "I just remember thinking, 'Please don't let that freezing water fall on me!'"

"But the Young Master said it would help us," Mal countered, "meaning it would come to our aid – at our command. It can't happen only when we're scared. There must be more, another way to activate our gifts."

"The water obeyed me this morning," Ari recalled. "Let me try." He walked to the water's edge. Damp sand shifted beneath his feet and the cool liquid crept over his sandals, seeping between his toes. Ari stretched out his arms and squinted his eyes, trying to think powerful, commanding thoughts. Maybe there was a special word he needed to use. *Move*, he thought at the water. His feet remained wet. The waves continued to lap happily at the shoreline. He thought about what had worked earlier.

"Go away!" he cried and flung his left arm out and to the side. Still, nothing. Come to think of it, that was a really horrible idea anyway. What if all the water had gone away simply because he'd commanded it? Where would it have all gone? And, if his feet were still wet (he'd checked, they were), this apparently wasn't working. He shook the sodden granules from his feet and relocated to drier ground.

"Maybe we're going about it all wrong," Mal deduced. "Maybe it really will come to us when we need it. Can't say we really need it right now …" he shrugged and trailed off helplessly.

"So, we've made no progress," Martha sighed, dejectedly.

"None at all," chimed in Ari.

"We're back where we started," Mal agreed.

Chapter 10

If I could do anything, be anything, be anywhere ...

They walked along the beach, close to the shoreline, talking. Martha found it a little hard to keep up with the boys. They were so caught up in their ponderings that they would have forgotten all about her, if that were possible. Martha wasn't about to let them forget about her. She wanted her voice to be heard. So she kept up a steady stream of running commentary as she aired her thoughts aloud. Between the three of them, there was a lot of "Hmmm ... I wonder" that went nowhere and got them no closer to an answer.

Soon after, boredom kicked in and Martha gave up really trying to be included in their conversation. She began to skip and hop among the rocks. She realized, at that moment that she was happy. Why? Because for once, she felt big. She had not one, but TWO powers! Wait – *Two*? Her shoulders slumped in defeat, and she came to a standstill as it occurred to her; two powers that she had no idea how to access.

"You know," she heard Mal say, catching the tail end of their discussion, "the problem is that these 'powers' are no good!" he vented. "What good is the 'power of wind' anyway?"

"Truly," Ari agreed, at least, in this. "I mean, if you're going to get a power, why not something wonderful like the power to move across the ages?"

"Yes," Mal seconded. "Then we could go back and forth in time!" He was warming up to his subject now. "What if you could meet someone from the past – anyone – who would it be?"

"That's easy," Ari said excitedly. "'I'd want to meet the Warrior King!"

"What?" Mal contested, "I'd rather see the man he beat! We learned about him at school. They said he was *huge*!"

"Well, Mama says that he was beautiful," piped in Martha.

"Beautiful? You mean the one he beat?" Mal questioned, incredulously.

"No! I mean, yes! The Warrior King!" Martha replied, confused at their exchange and exasperated that Mal didn't try harder to keep up. "They say he was beautiful and dreamy and strong ..." She sighed and trailed off as she ran out of adjectives to describe him. Her own eyes took on a dreamlike quality as she continued her rambling. "Oh, and fearless!" she suddenly remembered.

Smacking sounds drew her attention and brought her out of her reverie. She turned to find the source of the noises. Mal and Ari were play fighting with sticks for swords. As it turned out, Ari was pretty good, for he disarmed Mal quickly.

Thinking to join in their play, Martha ran across the sand to pick up Mal's "sword." She had nearly caught up to them when her sandal caught on a small stone nearly buried in the sand. Martha lost her balance, and her run gave her momentum. She couldn't stop. Falling forward, her arms flailing before her, she instinctively tried to grab on to something or someone to stop her fall. Her right hand caught Ari on his wrist, and her left landed on Mal's upper leg. Though small, she managed to send them all tumbling forward as they crashed into the tall, wet grass. Wait – grass?

Chapter 11

Far, far from home …

Mal rose slowly to his feet and looked at the lush, green valley all about them, bemusedly. Somehow, they were no longer at the beach. Ari popped up like an ostrich next to Mal, craning his neck all around to see. He scratched his head. Martha got up last, slowly, taking in her surroundings.

Tears threatened to spill over, and her voice quavered when she spoke: *"Where are we?"*

"Samson, NO!" A male voice called from their left. The threesome turned just in time to see a large shepherd's dog come bounding towards them at full speed. A boy followed quickly after him. Thank goodness the dog was friendly. He wagged his tail so hard that his entire body shook from the effort. He was full of energy and bounced back and forth between them exuberantly, before finally settling on Martha. He jumped up on her and put his front paws on her shoulders, nearly bowling her over. She could hardly breathe as Samson licked her face so enthusiastically that she temporarily forgot that she was near tears just a few moments earlier.

"Samson, DOWN!" the boy called, trying to restore some semblance of order. "Now!" he said, this time more firmly, accompanying the command with a tug on the dog's scruff. Samson yielded and sat back on his haunches. The boy rubbed the dog vigorously, distracting him while the children took this opportunity to look over the stranger. As they sized him up, warily, he did the same.

His clothing appeared to be similar to their own but somehow, different – more rustic in design. He wore a simple tunic, as did they, and a mantle of goat's hair overlaid it. The bottom of his tunic was tucked into his girdle to make it easier to move about. Sandals and a staff completed his outfit. They determined from his crooked staff that he was a shepherd. The boys narrowed their eyes at the newcomer trying to determine if this was a good development or not so good. No one spoke for a moment, but their thoughts could easily be discerned by the looks on their faces.

Oh, he's just a shepherd! Mal thought, dismissing the boy as harmless. He felt sure he could take him if need be. To be on the safe side, he casually readied himself for battle, planting his feet and standing with a wide stance, fists gathered loosely at his side. He cast a speculative glance at the newcomer that contained a hint of suspicion and warning, just in case he got any ideas. Mal puffed out his chest to make himself appear larger.

He's about our age, thought Ari, feeling a bit friendlier about the encounter. Although, upon closer inspection, he could have been easily a few years older. He was as tall as Mal (who was tall for his age) though, not as stout. Ari wondered, fleetingly, if the boy could provide some help or insight as to what had happened to them. At the very least, he appeared harmless; otherwise, he could have ordered his dog to *eat them* instead of calling him off. Samson was just that big. In appearance, Samson looked like your typical shepherd dog, mostly white with a few tan markings and a tail that curved upward. But he did seem abnormally big, hence the name, Ari thought dryly. Maybe he was a mixed breed.

Martha took one look at the boy and inwardly sighed. He was absolutely lovely. *What a beautiful boy*, she thought. He was pretty enough to be a girl but rugged, too. You could tell he spent a lot of time outside in the fields. His skin was brown from days spent under the sun, and his body was wiry and strong. But his hair – it could have rivaled Martha's for beauty. It was thick and full and hung past his shoulders. It was a bit matted, but even in its unkempt state, you couldn't ignore it. Martha concluded that he likely didn't take very good care of it, being a boy and all. He wore a simple band tied about his head to keep it out of his eyes.

After assessing the situation, Mal decided the boy was not a threat. He exhaled and relaxed, "I'm Mal." He made further introductions, "This is Ari and Martha." Mal gestured to his companions as he spoke.

"I'm sorry about that," the young shepherd apologized. "Samson is not usually like that with strangers." He looked at Martha and smiled contritely. "I don't know what got into him."

"Maybe you can help us," Mal broke in when it seemed the young shepherd would make further apologies. "We seem to have lost our way." *To say the least,* he thought. Maybe this fellow could provide some answers. Before he could continue, Ari nudged his arm and muttered under his breath. Mal turned to him questioningly, but Ari was suddenly preoccupied with a bird in the sky.

"Look at it fly." Ari followed it with his finger in a path across the sky. Mal glowered at Ari as if he'd lost his mind.

Ari knew he looked crazy – nothing new about that. He'd meant to distract Mal from his question. As Ari took in his surroundings, he noticed that, not only were they in a green valley, but they were also very far away from *any* beach or sand. The air even smelled different, like the forest instead of the sea. Foliage, grass and trees, as far as the eye could see.

Off in the distance, he saw a flock of sheep grazing and guarded by dogs. They clearly were nowhere near the place where they'd begun. And this shepherd boy – although his look was similar to theirs, Ari perceived there was something different about him. They'd all been transported somewhere, Ari figured, likely to do with their new "powers." They needed to sort this out before talking it over with a stranger or else Ari wouldn't be the only one who was thought of as crazy.

But before any of them could formulate a response, the dogs began to bark and growl frantically. Samson took off to join them as the children looked for the source of the ruckus. They saw a large, shaggy figure moving through the trees. Martha gasped. Ari froze. Mal threw his arms out on either side, barring his companions from going forward. The young shepherd dodged Mal's arm and ran toward the commotion, yelling with all his might. He thrust his shepherd's staff in the air as he raced, ready to challenge the great bear that emerged from the woods, bent on attacking his sheep.

Chapter 12

Battle of the Bear

With a war cry, the young shepherd flung himself down the hill, intent on protecting his flock. The children followed on his heels as quickly as they could, but the shepherd was faster and more familiar with the terrain. He soon left them behind. As the shepherd boy approached the bear, he yelled and swung the staff with all of his might, trying to distract the predator and draw his attention away from the young lamb it was after. He hit and poked the bear with the staff as the dogs lunged and nipped at the bear's heels. It was quite a show and, initially, the young shepherd seemed to be winning. Then the beast turned swiftly and swiped at the shepherd with his huge paw. The young man caught the blow in his side, and he was flung against a tree.

All of the creature's concentration was now focused on the young boy, who lay on the ground, stunned, dazed and unable to defend himself. He struggled to get up, gasped and then clutched his side. The bear reared up on his hind legs and loomed above the young boy, preparing to attack. Samson jumped between the two of them, snarling and with teeth bared, to defend his master. The dog advanced on the bear, trying to make him retreat. It seemed to work, at first, but then the bear backhanded the dog, too. Samson yelped as he took the hit but got back up, albeit slowly. With a menacing rumble in his chest, he leapt at the bear.

HELP! Martha said to herself, realizing what was about to happen to the beautiful boy, right before their eyes. The injured Samson was no match for the enraged, hungry animal. The pack of dogs encircled the bear from behind, baiting him, nipping at his heels and trying to draw his focus away from the young shepherd and the embattled dog. But the brutish creature threw them off, eyes only for his fallen prey. Martha screamed as she raced through the undergrowth.

"Noooooooo!" She cried out in panic. The tips of her fingers began to tingle. A fiery globe descended from the sky, plummeting at an alarming rate. It soared past Ari and Mal and caught Martha from behind, momentarily lifting her off her feet and causing her back to arc while she was airborne. She glowed all over with an ethereal light, consumed, but not. When Martha gained her feet again, she found she was still running. On impulse, she flung her hand out, towards the boy and his protector. The fire flowed smoothly, fluidly from her hand in the shepherd's direction. It hit the ground with a *whoosh*, surrounding both boy and dog and formed an impenetrable barricade. Terrifying to behold, the blaze grew wide and taller than the bear, causing him to recoil. In the face of such intense heat, the savage animal reared up and back on his hind legs.

Knowing he had been thwarted, the bear growled his frustration and began to back away. The dogs sensed his retreat and renewed their attack, ferociously. All, that is, but Samson, who'd remained at his master's side and was sealed in by the wall of fire. The pack of canines pressed their advantage until they drove the bear away. Mal and Ari slowed their run as they took in the scene, their jaws dropping in astonishment. Dimly, they were aware of Martha, still racing, still screaming.

The fire died as she approached the, now unconscious, shepherd boy. Martha ran to him and collapsed at his side. She was hysterical and mortified by what had almost happened and by what she had *done*. Adrenaline continued to surge through her veins, and she felt glad and half deranged, all at the same time. She was victorious! He was almost killed by the bear! Overwhelmed by the enormity of her conflicting emotions, she continued to scream and sob as tears ran down her face. Ari reached her first and knelt by her side. He didn't try to interrupt but instead, waited.

"Hey," he said finally, gently, when she paused to draw a breath in preparation for another bout of screaming. He drew the word out. "Hey there," he tried again, squeezing her shoulder to get her attention, trying to bring her back to them. "You don't need to do that. You don't want to do that." He spoke to her in a soft, sing-songy voice, calming her. "All is well. You saved us. See?" He pointed to Mal, who lowered himself next to the young shepherd, checking him while Samson licked his master's face.

"Arrrgh ...?" The scream died in Martha's throat before it could reach full volume. She focused on Ari and her eyes lost their glazed look. Then she was back with them, still crying and trembling, but no longer screaming.

"Oh, Ari!" She catapulted herself into his arms, rocking him back on his heels. "I was so afraid!" She sobbed as Ari patted her back, nodding in sympathy and comforting her. He let her cry and held her while she trembled. He knew how she felt. One thing he understood, all too well, was crazy.

****

A lone figure stood on the beach, over the area where Mal, Ari and Martha were last seen. Drawn there by the pulse of power, he felt its signature in the atmosphere. He knelt down and scooped up some of the sand where Martha had stubbed her toe. Eyes like those of a cat burned golden-green from underneath the hood of his cloak. He lifted his head; a forked tongue snaked out delicately, and tasted the air. He sniffed and turned his head. As he smiled in satisfaction, it was a beautiful smile with perfect teeth.

"Ahhhhh ..." he said to himself. Not only did he know where they were, he knew when.

Chapter 13

A New Friend

"I'm going to kill that bear," the boy muttered as he regained his bearings. He shook off his grogginess and tried to sit up. The children had taken turns watching over him, and his flock while he was recuperating. Mal looked at him doubtfully.

"You can't kill a bear," Mal scorned, curling his upper lip in disbelief.

"How?" Ari questioned simultaneously. Both eyebrows lifted inquiringly. Not that he wanted any part of killing the bear, he was just curious.

"I don't know how, yet. But I will when the time comes," the shepherd replied. "I must kill him. He's become too aggressive and too dangerous. He has no fear. I was only trying to drive him away but he nearly killed me. If it hadn't been for your help, I might now be dead."

Mal and Ari gave an, *it was nothing* shrug. They tried to downplay their role in his rescue because, truly, it was Martha who had saved him. Also, they didn't know how much he saw or remembered about what had happened.

"I owe you my life," the shepherd said, placing his right hand over his heart. As he said it, he made it sound formal, like a pledge, an oath of loyalty. He bowed his head from his sitting position. "Is there anything I can do for you? Are you lost? Hungry? I can take you to my father's house." He looked up eagerly and then caught himself. "But wait, we haven't truly met. I am called David." He stretched out his hand to Mal, then Ari, clasping their hands in a very solemn and adult manner. "Anything I can do for you, everything I have, is yours."

****

Martha insisted on taking her turn watching the sheep as she had decided that of the three of them, she could definitely take care of herself. Martha had already fallen in love with the young lamb the bear had been after and had taken to petting it. The feeling was mutual for the lamb followed her around like a puppy.

If David thought it strange that such a small girl could be left by herself to that duty after the bear attack, he didn't question it. He seemed to know that the three children were *other* than they seemed. Samson's reaction to them was also quite telling. His dog was not usually so friendly with strangers. However, David did question just how his rescue took place.

"What happened after I fell unconscious? How did you save me?" he'd asked when he felt more stable.

But the boys demurred, telling him that the dogs had done all the work (partly true) in driving the bear off. They played up Samson's part and told him how the dog stood his ground against the bear. David smiled and ruffled Samson's fur, hugging him close. Even now, after the danger had passed, Samson refused to leave his master's side.

Satisfied that they'd successfully changed the subject, the boys began to make plans to stay the night. They reasoned that they could hardly leave David as he had not fully recovered from the bear attack. (To David, they offered the excuse that they were simply travelers who'd lost their way.) More truthfully, they really couldn't leave because they had no place to go, although they didn't think it necessary to let on to David. Besides, he'd already offered them his hospitality and had left off asking questions that the children clearly didn't want to answer.

Mal and Ari thought they were getting more adept at deflecting David's questions. They kept diverting his attention elsewhere and before long, he just stopped asking. In reality, the young shepherd had picked up on their reluctance to answer, so he left off pressing for more details. It might be considered impolite to continue to inquire; they were, after all, his guests. It was the least that he could do, considering they'd saved his life. Although he didn't voice further inquiries aloud, he still wondered.

As the evening waned, it foretold a beautiful night. The sky was clear, and the temperature seemed just right, not too hot, nor too cold. A gentle wind played about them, stirring the air and cooling their skin as they worked. They set up camp for the night near a small clearing where there were fewer rocks and the sheep could continue to graze.

The children gathered wood to build a fire, but they didn't stray too far. The memory of their encounter with the bear was still fresh in their minds. They left the building of the fire to David. Starting a fire from scratch could be challenging, but the young shepherd had an experienced hand and soon got the fire going. He made it look easy – rubbing the pieces of wood between his hands quickly until the wood began to smoke. He gently blew on the wood, encouragingly. The kindling soon caught fire and began to make crackling sounds.

As the smell of smoke permeated the air, the sight and sounds actually made Martha a little homesick. About this time, she would normally be helping her mother to finish preparations for dinner. David bent to his task, adding more fuel to feed the fire while explaining that it would likely keep more predators at bay. But they would still keep watch during the night, just in case.

Then their young host produced several fish, strung together on a line, which he had caught earlier in preparation for his supper. He seemed to have rebounded quickly from his encounter with the bear. He had lined the area under the fire with rocks and fashioned a spit to roast the fish. Along the hot rocks, he laid a small supply of root vegetables, wrapped in leaves and herbs he carried in his bag. The smells emanating from the roasting vegetables and fish were so tantalizing, they made Martha's mouth water. She suddenly realized she was *so* hungry!

She checked her own belongings for provisions, wanting to add to the meal. Ari and Mal did the same. Before long, they all sat down to a well-rounded dinner of fish and vegetables, supplemented with bread, cheese, dates and figs. The children found they were famished after all the drama wrought that day and fell upon the food, making quick work of it. When they'd finished, they sat back, rubbing their stomachs in a satisfied, contented sort of way. A good meal went a long way towards making their harrowing day better.

David rose and herded his flock into a natural pen fashioned of boulders, rocks and branches, to discourage further predators. The children helped until, at last, he ushered them in, too. In true shepherd fashion, he laid his mantle on the ground and made his bed in the opening of the pen. David, himself, was the gate and any beasts of prey would have to get past him. The children sat near the mouth of the enclosure with David and settled in for the night.

All fell quiet, but it was of a calming sort that just grew. For a while, they sat, paying attention to all of their senses – the sounds of small animals rustling through the grass, the sight of the fire crackling nearby, the delectable smell of the remains of their dinner. Then their eyes beheld the night sky. It was clear, cloudless and decorated with stars. In the quietude of the forest and with no other distractions, they could truly appreciate its handiwork. True, they could see the same sight as they lay on the roof of any of their homes. Tonight, however, seemed different. Looking at the vast expanse of sky stretched before them made them feel humbled. Each star was a pinprick of light on a sea of darkest night. Were they deliberately hung there or haphazardly flung there? No matter, for they were beautiful.

"It looks like a curtain of stars, hanging in the sky," remarked Martha pensively, breaking into the stillness.

"It reminds me of the promise made to our forefathers," said Mal. "*Avraham* was told that his descendants would outnumber the stars."

"All that from one man?" joked Ari to dispel the serious undertone of the conversation. Although, in truth, he felt like one of those stars – just one among many.

With the silence dispelled, David got up and put more wood on the fire. Then he reached for his shepherd's bag and pulled out a stringed musical instrument, a small lyre of sorts. He sat down with his back against the wall of the enclosure and began to strum on the weathered instrument lightly. A hush fell again as the children listened to its harp-like quality. The sounds it emitted at David's expert hands were so sweetly inspiring, that Martha wanted to weep. Moved to contribute, Ari pulled out his little wooden flute with dual pipes, which always hung from a leather strip on his neck, and accompanied David. They all sat or lay in their various reposes around the fire, thinking how perfect a night. Then David began to sing. His voice, like his countenance, was beautiful, as well. He sang of the beauty of creation, of the wonder of man and the One True God who made them all:

> *When I look at the sky, which you have made,*
>
> *At the moon and the stars, which you set*
>
> *In their places with your own fingers*
>
> *What am I, a mere mortal, that you think of me;*
>
> *Or human beings, that you care so much for us?*
>
> *You have made us inferior only to yourself;*
>
> *You have crowned us with glory and honor.*
>
> *You made us rulers over everything you made;*

Giving us dominion over all of your creation:

Sheep and cattle, and the wild animals too;

The birds and the fish and the creatures in the seas.

O LORD, our Lord, O LORD, our Lord,

Your greatness is evidenced all over the world!

"What a lovely song," Martha commented as David finished his song and trailed off, still humming. She thought the song was simply beautiful. It had a familiar ring to it, but she still asked, "Did you write that?" David nodded in response, plucking at the strings of his lyre and picking out poignant notes.

Just as the silence began to grow around them again, he started up another song. This time, he picked up the pace and sang a silly little ditty about a fat farmer with a thin wife and a lazy child and a three legged dog. It was uproariously funny; so much so, that it was all the kids could do to keep up and come in with the chorus. Ari gave up trying to play his pipe and soon they were all holding their stomachs and sides as they gave in to the laughter. For the moment, they forgot about being in a strange place, far from home. For a short time, they even forgot about the bear attack. They just enjoyed being present and in the company of their new friend.

Something in the surrounding bushes caught Martha's attention, causing her mood to sober up quickly. Eyes, like the eyes of a cat, golden-green and gleaming, peered out at them from the woods. Martha sat up straighter. Her own eyes got wide when she thought she heard a low growl. She jumped a little and blinked. The eyes were gone. The boys quieted, noting her reaction.

"What? Martha, what's wrong?" Mal asked.

"Are there lions here?" She gulped, and looked around nervously. "In this forest?"

"Yes," David answered, "but they don't usually come near the fire – it pretty much keeps all but the most determined predators away." As he said this, he got up and added more wood to the fire, just to be safe. "Why, what did you see?"

"I thought I saw eyes, golden eyes, and I think I heard noises, too. A-and a rumbling sound," she stammered. "Didn't you? Did you hear it?" Martha was wary. Her ears strained to hear more telltale signs of a lion.

No, the boys hadn't heard. Likely because, at the time, they were still laughing. Or perhaps, because there was nothing to hear. Quite possibly, she'd imagined it all. She felt suddenly very tired. Her mind was playing tricks on her. It had been a long and exhausting day, filled with far too many events to digest. She was simply overwrought and needed some rest. Besides, she thought determinedly, no lion had better mess with her tonight. In her present mood, he might just get *burned*. Her fingers flexed and stretched, on impulse. As she drifted off to sleep, she imagined she felt a trickle of power, ready to do her bidding at the mere thought. The very idea comforted her immensely.

Unknown to them, golden-green eyes watched while they slept …

Chapter 14

The next day dawned clear and beautiful. The boys rose with David while Martha continued to sleep. She slept like a person drained from the previous day's activities. Mal and Ari hadn't gotten the opportunity to talk to Martha about her power and how it was activated. They halfheartedly attempted to help David with the flock, but in reality, their minds were elsewhere. They were eager to explore their surroundings now that it was fully light. They still didn't know much about where they were.

David sensed the boys were consumed with weightier things than tending sheep, so he waved them off, urging them to stay close. But Mal and Ari wandered a little deeper into the forest. They talked as they walked, turning here and there as they felt so inclined. Ari almost got the sense that he was being led.

Turn here, or *go there* he imagined he heard in his mind. Or was it only his imagination? He argued with himself the entire time – *why should I turn here?* Was he speaking to himself or was there another voice? Yet, obediently, he turned and went as directed, wending his way through the trees. Mal followed, too, meandering along without question. He wasn't sure why, either.

"So ... that was Martha's gift at work," Mal brought up the subject that was foremost in both of their minds.

"It was truly ... amazing!" Ari gushed in admiration. Ari still couldn't believe what he'd seen. The two boys wondered when their own gifts would be revealed and if it would be in a similar fashion. They began to reflect on the memory of Martha's demonstration of power and what it could mean for them. Each lost in his thoughts; they absentmindedly followed a trickle of water. It soon grew, lengthening and winding until it led to a dark bed of water. It was wide now, far too wide to jump over, and they were hesitant to wade into the murky water because they couldn't fathom its depth.

"There's got to be a way across," Mal muttered. They looked further up the stream to find an easier place to traverse, hoping to see if it would narrow or if some type of bridge existed.

"Do you think ..." Ari's eyebrows flashed, and he gave Mal a look. Mal's eyes widened as it occurred to him, too. Maybe this was *their* opportunity to unlock the power of their gifts. Neither of them had thought to turn around and go back to the camp. Could it be they had been led here for a reason? They had been drawn, unavoidably, to this place and knew intuitively they *had* to try to get to the other side. The question was: how? Ari scratched the top of his head as he pondered. Mal rubbed his jaw and did the same. Hmmm.

Suddenly, Mal's eyes lit up – he had an idea! "I wonder ..." he mumbled to himself. He walked over to a young tree that had been nearly uprooted – whether by a storm or because it was half dead, he wasn't certain. It was already leaning pretty badly and partially broken at the base. He was big enough, strong enough, he thought. He could possibly push the tree with enough force to completely dislodge it. The small tree might prove just long enough to use as a bridge to cross over.

Mal pushed, testing the strength of the tree and grunted. The tree didn't budge. He stepped back to examine the angle of the tree, planted his feet more firmly and tried again. Still, nothing happened. Mal looked around for something to help dislodge the tree. He found a big rock and a thick, heavy branch. He placed both at the base of the tree and tried to use them as leverage to force the tree to move. Still didn't work.

Mal grumbled aloud, tongue-in-cheek, "Some tremendous *strength* would be really useful right now. It'd be very *helpful*." He announced to the sky, not truly believing it would work, "Whenever you're ready." All he got in response was the birds calling to each other through the trees. Maybe he should try a different approach.

"Power of the wind, come to my *aid!*" Mal said suddenly as he hurled himself at the tree with all of his might. He hit it with a thud. Not even a creak or groan came from the tree. He growled to himself. Just how did Martha activate her power anyway? He stepped back, yelled at the tree and ran at it again, full force, leading with his shoulder.

"Help meeeeee!" he cried as he ran. Mal hit the tree with an "oomph!" for his trouble, bounced off it and hit the ground. Frustrated, he got up and began to attack the tree, beating and punching it, punishing it for refusing to cooperate.

"Argh!" Mal yelled, hacking and chopping at the tree with the side of his hand. The tree was unmoved, but he was breathing hard from the exertion. His hands were red from the pounding, so he kicked the tree instead, which really hurt his toe. So he stomped the bottom of his foot against the tree. OW! He knew he would feel the effects in his body later. Still, he didn't give up.

Ari looked on at the growing spectacle – the battle between Mal and the tree and thought, *that's got to hurt*. Obviously, brute force would not work. He assumed the pose that people take on when they are deep in thought – one hand on his elbow, the other on his face, stroking his upper lip and chin. He thought to himself, it *can't* be this hard. Martha had somehow found a way, but it couldn't be the only way. The Young Master wouldn't have left them without resources. At that moment, Ari recalled something his mom always said - *ask a question and you'll get an answer*. So he simply asked … how?

Before he could fully formulate the question, the answer came to him, quick as a wink – faster than he could think. He knew the answer didn't come from his own consciousness. Abruptly, and for no apparent reason, he somehow knew how to proceed. He didn't want to tell Mal what he was about to do because he would feel foolish if it didn't work. So he walked right past Mal, and to the water's edge while Mal continued to pummel the tree.

Ari stood at the lip of the water; he centered himself, closed his eyes and took a deep breath. Feelings akin to those he'd felt last night as he watched the stars, and the weight of his own insignificance amongst so many of this vast creation, flooded him. But to the Creator, he knew, he was important. He felt, in some way, in tune with his surroundings. The water, the trees and sky – he was connected to the source of them all, and he knew that their genesis was the same as his own. He looked down at the brownish water, lifted his arms at the elbow and made a pushing motion with the palms of his hands, forward, then out as he said to the water, "MOVE."

A shaft of sunlight fell across the water, turning it a beautiful, crystal clear blue. Now, Ari could see the bottom of the river and the rocks lying there. He watched in wonder as an assortment of small fish swam by. Then, to his increasing astonishment, the water began to ripple at the base. He marveled as the water followed the exact pattern of the motion of his hands – forward then out – until it formed a low wall of water on each side of a now, perfectly dry river bed. Ari had created a pathway right through the stream. He got it right! Outwardly, his expression appeared dumbfounded, but inwardly, his mind was doing leaps, jumping up and down. He couldn't hold back the happy sound; it escaped, drawing Mal's attention.

"Mal," Ari breathed reverently, in awe of himself and the power he now wielded. "I did it." Mal stopped cold at the sight, stunned. Ari's gift worked!

"Yahhhh!" Mal shouted and ran at Ari, who nearly ducked because he didn't know what to expect. Mal grabbed Ari in a bear hug, temporarily lifting Ari off his feet. Ari's grimace turned into a grin as Mal dropped him back on his feet. Then, they screamed at each other, jumping about and doing a celebratory dance.

Ari calmed, looking down at the newly created "highway." The water foamed happily, bubbling and rippling on each side of the pathway, in synchronization with his mood. Mal grew quiet, too. He came and stood by Ari's side. Mal put his arm on Ari's shoulder and squeezed, encouragingly. He was actually happy for Ari. He was. Yet, Mal's inability to activate his own gift was starting to put a damper on his spirits.

"My friend," Mal began but became even more subdued, his elation over the act quickly deflating. Still, he wanted to be supportive, so he gave himself a mental shake and tried again. He patted Ari on the back. "You … you did it." But Ari hadn't noticed Mal's hesitation. His hearing halted when Mal had first spoken. And Ari's heart warmed at that word, *friend*. He hadn't had a friend in what seemed like a long while.

Together, the two boys ventured to the other side.

Chapter 15

Martha was awakened by something wet and rough on her face. Stroking, no, licking her face – over and over. She opened her eyes cautiously and squinted at the sun shining brightly overhead. Where was she? She was lying on her back in a bed of grass and looking up at a clear blue sky. She blinked rapidly and put out her arm in an attempt to shield her eyes from the sun's glare. But she needn't have bothered, for a little lamb's head popped directly in her view, blocking the brightness. Martha smiled and remembered.

"Hello, Mary," Martha said quietly and reached out to pet the small lamb. The lamb nudged Martha insistently with her muzzle as though saying: GET UP! Martha laughed softly and sat up. She looked around for her companions. Mal and Ari weren't anywhere to be seen. But she saw David, standing a way off, talking with a young man. The man looked somewhat like

David but older. Of course, not nearly as handsome, Martha noted. A mule stood nearby, grazing on the grass at the foot of a tree. Martha caught snatches of their conversation:

"Now?" David asked.

"Yes, Father says he needs you to come home," the man replied. He spoke very slowly and carefully, like he was trying hard to be patient and wanted to be sure David understood.

"How soon?" David ignored his tone.

"As soon as possible; we have a guest, and your presence is *required*," his brother said, in his best snooty tone. He finished with a mocking little bow.

David rolled his eyes and shook his head. His brother could be such a jester at times.

"I'll start back today, El. I should be home by tomorrow evening," David said.

"Good. I'll give Father the news so that he'll know when to expect you," The man gathered the reins of his mule, mounted and rode away without even so much as noticing Martha, who was still sitting on the ground. David turned at that moment and saw her sitting there, watching.

"Good morning, Martha," he said and smiled. Martha smiled back her greeting. She sighed, inwardly. He really was beautiful, she thought dreamily.

****

"So ..." Mal swallowed his pride and finally asked, "How did *you* do it?" He was still feeling a little envious. He just HAD to know.

"Well," Ari replied, "I just suddenly *knew*." He tapped a finger to his head, indicating he thought the knowledge just dropped down in there. "No – wait ... uhm ... let's go back. FIRST," he clarified, "I asked the question – *how*? And then, before you knew it, I KNEW it!" He grinned at his own wordplay.

Ari was genuinely trying to be as helpful as he could. He could tell that Mal was a little disgruntled at being left out so far. He tried to be sensitive to Mal's predicament and give as much information as possible so that Mal could find a way to access his gift, too. Ari described to Mal the tingling feeling in his fingertips and the warmth on the back of his neck.

"Somehow, I felt HELP had arrived – if that makes sense," Ari explained. He was on a cloud, still dizzy with his success. Mal nodded but inwardly, he was shaking his head. No, it did NOT make sense! "Help" was a *feeling*? *Oh no*, he thought gloomily and rubbed his face with his hands, groaning mentally. He had a feeling that he was doomed.

****

Beyond the debut of Ari's gift, the remainder of their morning was uneventful. The boys soon tired of exploring and made their way back to camp. They'd managed to catch a few fish while exploring. Being the son of a fisherman, Mal always carried the means to do so – a bit of line and a hook – on his person. He waved Ari on with the fish, giving the excuse that he wanted to collect some firewood. In reality, Mal wanted to be alone.

Not that he begrudged Ari and Martha their gifts, but he was feeling a little sorry for himself and more than a little left behind. Rather than let his glum thoughts overshadow the joy of their gifts, he kept to himself. Why couldn't he get his gift to work for him? What would it take? He kicked up the dead leaves with his feet as he went, pondering the thought as he bent over to pick up fallen branches.

The sun felt warm and welcoming on his back. It relaxed him, and he felt a gentle breeze waft all around him. He straightened, closed his eyes and breathed deeply as he took it all in. It was always beautiful in a forest, surrounded by the trees and the canopy of leaves. It felt especially peaceful here, soothing his troubled spirit and his injured pride. Here, he found solace, and the sounds of the forest seemed to fall away. As he concentrated on the deep silence around him, he felt something tickle his ear. He ignored it. *Probably just a falling leaf*, he thought, and went back to enjoying his solitude.

The tickling started up again, this time, becoming more persistent. He partially opened his eyes, annoyed a little, at the distraction. *Maybe a fly or bug*, he thought as he waved the "bug" away. Mal didn't see anything, but the tickling stopped.

Suddenly, the wind became brisk and gusty. It stirred the carpet of dry leaves on the forest floor, causing them to rise and race around him in a circle. Mal heard the rustling of leaves – it was a loud roar in his ears. He raised his arms from his sides and watched in wonderment while the leaves swirled about him in a cyclonic fashion, surrounding him and sheathing his lower body in a column of leaves.

"W-what …?" Mal was head-to-toe warm, and his extremities tingled as it dawned on him – HIS GIFT! His gift had come for him. Faster and faster the leaves rushed around him. The tickling began at his ear again. Only this time, he knew it wasn't a bug or a fly. It was the wind, his gift, teasing him. He made a swishing motion with his hand, left to right, and the tickling ceased. The wall of swirling leaves collapsed. He turned his hand over and looked at his open palm and wondered, *hmmm* …

He waved his hand again, in the opposite direction, and the curtain of leaves began to rise once more, encircling his feet. *Oh*, he thought, *swish* on, *swish* off! He repeated the motions several times, just to be certain. *On, off. On, off.* Each time the wind responded and the rustle of leaves started up again. Then, he felt a little bump from behind, causing him to stumble forward a few steps – but he didn't fall, for the wind *caught* him. His body jolted as the wind lifted and carried him forward, just a little, playing with him.

These days, no one ever picked up Big Mal and the act made him laugh with pure delight. At last, he had his own gift, full of strength and power. This was a good development – very good, indeed.

Chapter 16

"I need to go home. I have been summoned by my father." Ari made it back to camp just as David was explaining to Martha. The shepherd boy looked from Ari to Martha and scratched his head. Then he rubbed his chin, seeming to search for an answer to a question yet unasked.

"You look worried – is there a problem?" asked Ari. He could see that his friend was concerned.

"Well," David said, "the problem is, I don't know what to do with you!" When Ari looked puzzled, David continued. "I don't want to leave you here to fend for yourselves. Would you all consider coming home with me?" He felt obligated to protect and care for his companions.

"We would be pleased to go home with you," Ari assured him, speaking on behalf of them all. Ari didn't foresee any problem with accepting David's invitation, as they had nowhere else to go. "It should be fine. Thank you for inviting us." Ari looked at Martha, who nodded in agreement. David breathed a sigh of relief.

"But wait – where is Mal?" David asked, noticing that Ari had arrived alone.

"Uhm ... he's nearby," Ari stalled. "He just wanted a little time to himself."

"Why? Is he alright?" David wondered about his new friend.

"Yes, he's fine – he was just feeling a little disappointed by something that happened." *Or failed to happen, as was the case*, Ari thought. He was purposely vague as he answered the question but cocked his eyebrow at Martha meaningfully. She looked back at Ari – her eyes full of questions that he knew he would have to answer later when they were alone.

For his part, David accepted Ari's explanation and decided to leave it at that. He at least understood that he wouldn't get anything more specific out of Ari. Although he was growing accustomed to their enigmatic answers, he didn't like the idea of Mal wandering alone, by himself.

"Let's go find him and tell him the news. Perhaps that will help to cheer him," David suggested. Ari and Martha readily agreed and Ari led the way, retracing his footsteps back to where he last saw Mal. As they approached, they could see Mal – he was giddy with excitement. He was laughing as though someone was teasing and playing with him, like he was being entertained. They watched as Mal was seemingly lifted off his feet by the wind and pushed forward. Ari gulped and looked at Martha.

"Ah, David ..." Ari turned and reached for David, belatedly, in an attempt to distract him. Words escaped him, and his voice trailed off. He had no explanation for Mal's feat of levitation. Martha's expression reflected Ari's own. It was universal for, *uh-oh*.

****

"What are you laughing at?" David asked from behind him.

"Huh?" Mal straightened and regained his footing as he slashed down with his right hand. He spun around abruptly to face the young shepherd, and tried hard to concentrate as he thought to himself – *off!* The leaves paused in mid air as the wind stopped altogether. They fell to the ground in a circular heap about his feet. *Off,* Mal pleaded silently as a few renegade leaves rustled and appeared to rise again. *Please stay OFF!* "What?" He said innocently and placed his hands behind his back, fidgeting a bit while he shuffled from one foot to the other. Getting caught by David was not such good news.

They all stood frozen in their little tableau for a moment, and Mal noted their reactions. Martha's face told all. Her mouth formed an "o" and her eyebrows were raised to her hairline. *Oooo* … she mouthed silently. Ari hung back and tried to give an inconspicuous, congratulatory grin. He made an affirming motion with his hand surreptitiously and winked. Rather than feel good, Mal's heart sank – it was an unspoken agreement between them that David wasn't supposed to know. He felt as though he had let Ari and Martha down by betraying their secret. He was supposed to be the *responsible* one.

"Be easy," David said, when he saw how jumpy and nervous Mal became. It was apparent in the way Mal kept opening and shutting his mouth that he was trying to devise an explanation for defying the laws of gravity. David held his hands out in a reassuring gesture. "I have already realized that you all are other than what you seem. And … I know why you're here."

"You do?" The question ricocheted between them as the three children whipped their heads towards David, considering his claim. *They* didn't even know why they were here. How could he know? *Whew*, Ari thought, relieved. He backed up and leaned against the nearest tree, his arms folded in front of him and waited for David to continue. This ought to be good.

"You are here to help me," David said, matter-of-factly. His tone implied that it was obvious. "At times, we entertain angels, and we don't even know it. Yes? You are angels." David had been taught that he should always be careful to entertain strangers because they could be angels in disguise. One never knew. He was adhering to the tradition and custom of his culture.

"No ..." Mal denied, drawing out the word, slowly. "We're not angels. At least, *I'm* not."

"Me, either!" Ari jumped in.

"Me, neither – WAIT! None of us are!" She scowled at Mal. Mal shrugged his shoulders and showed his teeth, looking sheepish. He was still trying to find a way out of the mess he'd created. If that meant implying that the others could somehow possibly be angels, so be it. He wanted to take the focus off himself.

"But you *are* here to help," finished David. When the three children continued to look puzzled, he explained. "*Adonai*, He is my Shepherd." He splayed his fingers on his chest as he said it as if the Great Shepherd belonged only to him. "He takes care of me. When there is danger, or I am in need of help, I can count on Him to care for me, just as I take care of my lambs. I think that is why He made me to watch over them so that I can know how He feels about me. He wants to provide for me, to guide me and keep me safe. He has great love for me."

David's eyes lit up, and as he continued to speak using flowery turns of phrases, it became apparent to the children that David was a bit of a poet. Spending time alone with his flock in the wilderness must have given him much insight into the

131

relationship between the Creator and his creation. It was evident that David felt he enjoyed a special bond with his Shepherd. He flung his arms out and spun around, kicking playfully at the dead leaves scattered about him. His upturned face was full of awesome wonder at all the Creator had done for him, for David, just because. The children beamed at his outburst. His joy was so genuine, it was contagious. He made them all long for the same kind of relationship.

"But David," Martha hated to interrupt his exaltation to point out the obvious. "Where is the danger?" She tugged on David's garment to get his attention and bring him back from his reverie. He turned in Martha's direction, still caught up in his devotions. His face gleamed and his spirit bubbled over with praise. "More importantly," she continued, "how do you think we can help?" Like Ari, Martha was interested in David's theory of why they had been brought there. He turned to face her at the question and froze. Her expression grew bewildered when she watched David's demeanor change. He looked past her now, not seeing her.

David walked past Martha and squatted near a dung heap on the ground. Then he looked up and saw claw marks on the nearby tree. He ran his fingers along the deep grooves cut into the bark, made by a large animal. He stood up slowly and looked at Martha.

"You were right, Martha," he announced, gravely. "I think we've found your lion."

She inhaled sharply and moved tentatively to David's side. Her eyes wildly scanned the foliage about them, searching rapidly for more signs of the fierce predator.

Chapter 17

"What is it?" Ari asked, peering down at the display.

"Cat scat," David replied, pointing to the pile of dung. "See the claw marks? He's marking his territory."

"What does this mean – what do we do?" Mal had no idea how they could defend themselves against a lion. *The real question is*, he thought, *what **can** we do*? But David's mind was elsewhere. His thoughts were of his flock, grazing helplessly in the meadow. Would Sampson and the other dogs be enough to keep a lion at bay?

"I must get back to my sheep," David said, his voice held a note of panic. He turned quickly, striding out of the forest. The discovery of the lion's droppings had put him on full alert. When he entered the clearing, he relaxed a little. His flock could be seen, grazing serenely in the meadow, from where they stood. Martha saw that the littlest one of them all, *her* lamb, had wandered off and was separated by some distance from the rest of the flock. She must have tried to follow Martha.

Suddenly, David broke into a run, and the boys followed suit. David fumbled with the pouch at his side as he ran while the dogs began to bark the alarm. Martha didn't have to wonder at all the turmoil, for she soon saw what they saw: the shadow of a great cat prowling the edge of the forest.

****

The huge feline emerged from the trees with a low growl, stalking slowly toward the defenseless little ewe. A sleek, full mane of majestic dark fur trailed to an end along the bony ridge that was prominent on his back. His muscles bulged as he padded forward, powerful limbs moving gracefully.

My lamb, Martha thought. She had begun to love it so much that she'd named it after her baby sister. Martha was welded to the spot in horror, unable to breathe. The lamb, too, seemed to mirror her actions and was unable to move. The lamb bleated helplessly, and Martha knew then, no one, no dog nor person would be able to reach the lamb in time.

"Oh no!" Martha cried and clutched her hands to her chest in terror as if to hold on to her own heart. She couldn't bear to watch, and she couldn't turn away. *Too late to run*, she thought. A voice, unbidden, spoke to her: *Hide*. She answered: *How? Where?* It came to her suddenly, and she knew. *Hide*, she commanded. She reached upward, toward a small cloud in the sky and pulled.

The smoky substance poured down from the heavens, rolling and billowing around the lamb, forming a hedge of protection. The cloud quickly engulfed the lamb, and she could no longer be seen. The lion, momentarily confused, shook his great mane and roared at the obstruction as the cloud roiled between them.

Mal and Ari drew up at the sight of the cloud on the ground, but David kept running and yelling. He barreled right past them, trying to gain the lion's attention. They wondered why when the immediate danger seemed to have passed. Although briefly put off because he couldn't see the lamb, David worried the lion could still *smell* the lamb and would not be deterred. The lion paced around the cloud. He put a paw through the cloud, testing its ability to keep him away from his chosen victim.

David found his slingshot in his pouch as he ran and fitted one of the stones he usually kept there. He swung it around in a circle overhead and let it fly. It hit the lion on the back, which had all the impact of a fly. David let loose another stone, this one, too, had little effect as it landed in the lion's mane. This succeeded, though, in getting the creature's attention. He turned to David, seeing new, easier prey.

He needs help, thought Mal. *Oh, right – HELP!*
"ON!" Mal cried and swished his hand, just as the lion leaped at David. A great gust of wind caught the lion in the chest and pushed him back on his hind legs so that he stood upright, like a man. The lion was held fast, immobilized in that position; his forelegs flailed helplessly in the air while he struggled. David looked over his shoulder at Mal and narrowed his eyes. Questions could come later, but there was no time to consider that now.

David stood before the hapless beast, now towering above him. The wind whipped about the shepherd and tore at his tunic, but David was not moved. Fitting a new stone to his sling, he wound it several times, gathering momentum with each rotation. Then he threw the stone with all his might. Aided by the wind, his aim was true. It hit the lion in the head, HARD! The lion went limp but hung there, suspended in the air. His forelegs dangled and ceased their struggle.

"Let him down!" David turned and yelled at Mal when he saw the lion would not fall. He waved his arms frantically. "Put him down, now! I must finish it!" He had to be certain it was over – he didn't even want to think about what would happen if the dangerous creature were to regain consciousness. Mal complied, waving his hand and uttering the command, *Off.*

The lion collapsed on the grass with a loud *Whump!* David dodged nimbly out of the way as the great beast landed, drawing his knife. He approached with care, but the lion did not stir. Doing the only thing he knew to do that would guarantee the safety of his flock and his new friends, he slew the lion. Martha looked away as he grabbed the creature by his shaggy beard.

****

"We must leave this place," David announced to his companions as he stood over the corpse of the vanquished carnivore.

Martha nodded in agreement as she approached the lamb, still encased in the cloud. But she had to get past the lifeless figure of her pet's would-be destroyer. Guardedly, she drew close to the animal, on the alert for any movement. Martha didn't trust that he was fully dead and could hardly believe the danger was over. Adrenaline coursed through her veins, displacing reason; she was still in fight or flight mode.

She calmed, though as she advanced on the small cloud. She watched as it transformed into a light fog, which quickly dispersed, leaving the baby ewe looking none the worse for the experience. Martha knelt down and hugged the lamb's neck, gratefully, while carefully keeping her back to David. She didn't want to see the creature that almost killed her pet, just yet, even though he'd already met his end.

Mal and Ari came and stood over the beast, too. They looked down into his glassy, golden eyes. He was huge! They looked at David filled with a new sense of admiration. He had killed a lion! With Mal's help, of course – *they had made quite a team,* Mal thought smugly.

David looked on the still form, feeling numb from the events. He didn't know what to make of it or how to think about it yet. He couldn't even focus on what he'd done. It was too mind-boggling. So he turned his attention to the next logical task. The carcass would attract unwelcome attention from scavengers, and David knew they should leave without delay. Yesterday, he was almost killed by a bear, and today, a lion. He didn't want to chance another encounter. He just wanted to get his guests and his flock to safety.

"Vultures will be coming soon," he remarked, shielding his eyes and looking at the sky. He imagined they were already gathering to claim their prize. "But we were leaving anyway. My father has asked for me. That is why I came to find you, Mal. We need to leave now if we're to return by tomorrow evening." Mal nodded in response. The attack of the lion had really brought home the need for them to find a safe haven. They were truly in the wilderness and far from home.

Ari felt a little paranoid, wondering what could possibly jump out at them next. This was the second attack in as many days. He felt protective of Martha, too. Not because she couldn't defend herself (she'd shown herself more than capable) but because of what she'd just witnessed. It was getting to be too much. She still seemed a little shook up. *Maybe she was a bit tender for this adventure,* he thought. He watched while Martha spoke to the little lamb in hushed tones, comforting both herself and the small creature. Together, the children helped David make his preparations.

As they were leaving, Martha dared finally to look over her shoulder at the would-be slayer. This lion must be one and the same as she glimpsed the other night. But his lifeless golden eyes seemed somehow different in the daylight. She shuddered.

Chapter 18

David herded his sheep in the general direction of his home while Mal, Ari and Martha helped where they could. A pall was cast over the group by the prior events, and it affected them all. Their journey had taken them to a strange, dangerous land, and they were really beginning to miss their homes. When and how could they return? They became more vigilant, watching for danger behind every tree, it seemed. David's thoughts were also of home. Why had his father sent for him? He was curious.

Traveling through a land full of heartbreakingly beautiful images, they barely took notice of the spectacular vistas they passed, so caught up were they in their dour musings. They journeyed in this way for a time, oblivious to the scenery, engrossed in their own thoughts.

Mal stuck close to David, feeling that he could identify with him more, being that they had killed a lion together, and all. His chest was a little puffed up at the part he'd played in the whole encounter. Martha and her wooly playmate were glued to each other, refusing to be parted. Ari, for his part, hovered over Martha as subtly as he could. He felt the desire to shelter her, similar to how she was protective of her lamb, but he didn't really see how he could do that. Their adventure, it seemed, was destined to be perilous.

The path was well worn; it was obvious that David and his animal companions were well acquainted with the way home. Ari decided all the gloom and doom was getting to him. Maybe he couldn't shield Martha, but he could find a way to take her mind off what she'd just witnessed. He just needed to lighten the mood. He remembered then that Martha had yet to see his gift in action. He never got the chance to tell her in all of the up*roar*, so to speak. So, he decided to have a little fun.

As they walked alongside a small, shallow stream, Ari paused to take in the view. Curious as to what drew Ari's attention Martha also stopped and came to stand by his side. The water moved constantly, gurgling and bubbling in places; it flowed over the pebbles and natural rock formations. Martha spied a miniature waterfall; she pointed it out to Ari, *oohing* and *aahing* at the sight. Ari seized his chance.

"Would you like to see my gift?" he asked, with a sidelong glance in her direction and a playful glint in his eye. Martha nodded in response, her eyes widening. Ari looked over his shoulder to make sure Mal and David weren't looking. He wanted this to be just for Martha. "Shhh ..." He put a finger to his lips, raising one eyebrow and pointing to the small waterfall. He extended his arm straight out in front of him and with his palm made a sweeping motion to one side. The water rushing over the fall suddenly changed course, following the direction of Ari's hand. It hung there, like a curtain that had been gathered to one side.

"Oh!" Martha gasped at the sight. She turned to Ari; her eyes grew even bigger at the manifestation of his gift. Then Ari took his other hand, pointed downward at the stream and made little squiggly motions with his forefinger. Martha watched as the surface of the stream followed the motions of his finger, creating tiny waves and ripples. Just then, something, some creature broke the surface, and began leaping and skipping across the water, playing. Ari's sharp intake of breath betrayed his surprise – his special water friend was back! And though Ari was a little taken aback at that revelation, he quickly recovered and continued the show for Martha's benefit. Martha clasped her hands together in delight and giggled.

"I saw that," Mal said from directly behind them. Ari and Martha were so immersed in their play that they hadn't heard Mal approach. Guiltily, Ari jumped. His hand dropped to his side, and the curtain of water fell with a splash before resuming normalcy. Ari turned to Mal with an unabashed grin and hunched his shoulders in a shrug. He'd just wanted Martha to see his power, too.

Mal rolled his eyes and shook his head at Ari. He knew Ari was showing off. But Ari was glad he'd shown her. He was unrepentant because Martha was cheered by the display. Although he was resigned to not being able to protect Martha, he would certainly do all he could to lift her spirits. Even Mal looked a little happier and relaxed. It was just the break they all needed.

As they turned to leave, Ari saw movement in his peripheral vision. He turned to find his water pal had separated from the water completely, leaving the stream altogether and was moving, gliding along on the ground behind him in an attempt to follow them.

"Argh!" Ari growled under his breath. "No!" he whispered frantically, "Go back!" Obediently, the water creature returned to its source. At the edge of the bank, it paused, performed a graceful pirouette and leapt into the water. It ended in a beautiful swan dive and was quickly absorbed back into the stream. "Hmph!" Ari said to himself in disbelief. Apparently, he wasn't the only one who liked to show off.

Mal heard Ari mumble and turned around with a questioning look. Ari just shook his head at Mal and held up his hand.

"Do not ask," Ari commented dryly, shaking his head. "You do not want to know." Inwardly, he groaned. *Why me?* He didn't see Martha with a little *fire* pal following her around.

****

David continued to drive his herd onward. So intent was he on reaching home that he'd missed the entire exhibition of Ari's gift. The children soon caught up to

David and began to bombard him with questions about his home life to pass the time. If they seemed reluctant to answer the same types of questions, David didn't let it bother him. Eventually, the subject turned to David's faith in the One True God. Did David know more about why they were brought here and how they were supposed to help?

"Well," David answered, "I know you are different from me because your clothes are slightly different. And the way you talk – it's the same language but not quite the same. Sometimes, it seems you're speaking a different language altogether! I know you don't want to or, maybe you cannot reveal too much, but tell me this – where are you from?" The children named their home town of Capernaum. David mulled the word over, testing the strange name with his tongue. "But wait! *Kefar Nahum*?" he exclaimed. The children nodded vigorously in assent, for that was the name of their village in the old tongue. "That is not far from here!"

Mal, Ari and Martha exchanged puzzled looks. Could it be that home was that close? That was exciting news. Maybe home was only a few days journey away! Ari was about to say just that, but as he opened his mouth to speak, Martha made a little negative motion with her head, and Mal gave him a look that meant: *We'll discuss this later.*

"As for helping me," David continued, "you may have already done so. I've never had to face down a lion. This time, I had to because he was threatening my flock. You all were also in danger. I defeated the lion with your help. That you are here is more proof that the Creator is ever watching me, that he loves me and that he will provide aid when I have need. I will never fear the lion again because of this. I know how to kill him, just where to hit him." He tapped his forefinger to his head, nodding. "And, I know God will help me."

Chapter 19

It was slow traveling with the flock. Near evening, David decided that they had traveled far enough from the lion's carcass to avoid further trouble. They were closer to his home but would still have to camp for the night. Even though the lion was out of sight, he was not very far from their thoughts. It was decided they would take turns watching the sheep so that they all could get a semblance of rest that night. The boys would take turns watching and let Martha sleep altogether because … well, because she was a girl! Martha didn't argue. Sometimes it was nice to be a girl.

She fell into an exhausted sleep, but her slumber was not restful, initially. It was fitful, and she tossed and turned most of the night. Images of a lion with ghastly, golden-green eyes and then the bear, too, haunted her dreams. She saw the lion, now scrawny and mangy-looking, stand up on his hind legs like a

151

man. He waved the bear on with his forepaw and pointed (for the paw then became a hand) in her direction. Martha whimpered in her sleep. It was truly terrible to behold. Just as the bear turned to her, revealing sharp claws and massive teeth, the images dissolved. She grew quiet and was able to rest, peacefully.

Martha woke the next morning to find the boys standing some distance off, talking animatedly and gesturing with their hands to something that lay beneath them. The sounds of their discussion must have filtered into her sleep and awakened her. Martha rose from her hard pallet on the ground and walked over to join them. She wanted to see what had gotten them all so worked up. The ground sloped where they stood; it was actually the edge of a small ravine. There, beneath them, in a little vale below, lay the prone figure of an enormous bear.

****

Martha stood there, aghast at the sight. She caught snatches of their conversation as her head spun, unable to comprehend fully what she saw before her. This was too incredible a feat – David killed the bear while they slept, all by himself! A thought occurred to her, causing her to wrinkle her brow and purse her lips in concentration. She grasped the tail end of a faint memory. A dream, she vaguely recalled, about the bear. But the dream didn't make sense; it wasn't possible that the lion could send a bear to attack them. The lion was now dead. She'd seen it with her own eyes. It didn't even warrant further speculation.

"Isn't that the same bear that attacked us before?" Mal asked. He couldn't be sure, but he thought he recognized the markings. The animal lay on his back, open-mouthed, its tongue lolling out the side. Mal resisted the urge to go and poke the bear with his toe.

"It's huge!" added Ari. He sure hoped it was the same bear, now dead. But it was unsettling to think that it had been following them.

"I did what I had to do," David said grimly, regarding the former threat. He seemed to take no pleasure in the death of the bear. "He was a danger to us all. He was a threat to my flock. He had no fear of man. And he was wandering too close to my home." He shook his head slowly. "I had no choice."

"How is this possible?" Martha wondered aloud, unnoticed until she had spoken. The boys turned their heads, as a unit, at the sound of her voice. Ari and Mal seemed to be equally awestruck by the turn of events as Martha. She knew it had to have happened while she slept. She could only assume they slept through it, too. Apparently, David had put the bear down quickly and quietly.

The three children were riveted as David told his tale of how he defeated the bear. On David's watch, towards dawn, the bear appeared. David rose and approached the bear, stealthily, trying not to wake or alarm them unnecessarily. As he drew close to the bear, it occurred to him that the bear could be beaten in a way similar to the lion. He readied his sling as he went. At that moment, the bear saw David and reared up on his hind legs, giving David a clean shot at his head. With one stone, David was able to take the bear down and it landed in the ravine. It was likely the sound of gathering crows that had awakened Martha, for they were raising quite an alarm. She turned from the grisly sight and walked away.

****

David shared his meager breakfast with them. It was simple: bread and cheese, along with some dried fruit and smoked fish. After a brisk clean up, they were soon traveling again. The boys walked alongside David, wanting to hear more of his pre-dawn battle with the bear. Martha kept close to them for a while, eyes searching. Their gruesome discovery this morning should have put her fears to rest, but she was unable to relax for fear of another attack. Her stomach grumbled for real food and the comfort of home. Oh, and a real chance to bathe, instead of just making do with splashes of water. Then the little lamb nudged her hand, insistently, wanting to be petted. It was enough to distract her gloomy, wandering thoughts and bring her attention back to the present.

"Truly, I've never come upon so much trouble, so many strange things at once," David was saying. Martha forced herself to pay attention. "First, you three appeared," he gestured to include them all. "Then, the bear AND a lion – and I was able to slay them *both*!" David pondered this thought for the first time; did the bear and the lion attack because of the children who accompanied him? Were they somehow after the trio? Or, was it as he'd originally thought – the threesome were angelic messengers sent to help him. Was he being prepared for something greater? Were they all? It seemed too much for coincidence.

Maybe all scenarios held elements of truth; it could be that his companions were messengers, *and* they were under attack. Something, it appeared, was intent on pursuing his fellow travelers – but to their deaths? *Not if he could help it,* he thought resolutely, and determined to try all the harder to protect them. These woods, which normally brought him such solace, were proving especially hazardous for his new friends. He needed to get them to his home and to safety. They had saved his life. He owed them that much.

Martha was so unnerved by this morning's events that she crept ever closer to David until he could hardly walk properly. She and the lamb continued to get underfoot. As she bumped into him once more, she looked up at him in chagrin and was about to apologize, again. She knew she was feeling extra babyish. The lamb was under her, and Martha was under David. But David just looked down at her and grinned. He understood. He reached out, tugged a thick braid of her hair, and gave her a reassuring hug.

Martha smiled back at him sunnily, warmed by his touch. She felt better. She felt safe.

"Look," David said and pointed before him, relief evident in his voice. When they emerged from the wooded area, the children caught their breath at the scene before them. "My *ba-yit.*"

Chapter 20

Sweet home …

It's not that David's home was grand. It wasn't. It was simple. The true beauty was in where it lay. The forest had been cleared back and as the sun set on the horizon, multi-colored rays of light fell on the homestead, illuminating the scene with an eerie glow. It was breathtaking. And it was the closest thing they had seen to a home, with all of its comforts, in a few days. The sprawling landscape included several rambling buildings to house different animals and store food. There was a big house (for he had many brothers) which seemed warm and inviting as it was lit from within.

On one side of the house, there was a huge pen to corral the sheep. Mal, Ari and Martha, helped David to herd the sheep into the pen, the dogs nipping at their heels. After being around David for a few days, they could tell that he wasn't his usual calm self. He seemed agitated, excited even. His movements became jerky and he appeared distracted. His fingers fumbled where they should have been nimble, and the latch on the gate proved especially troublesome before it was opened. David kept looking towards the big house. When it became apparent to all that he couldn't focus because he was too anxious to see his father, Mal spoke up.

"Just go! We'll finish for you," Mal reassured him.

David gave him a grateful look and took off, walking quickly before giving up and breaking into a run. A big grin stretched across his face. He was glad to be home. David burst into the front door of the house calling, "Father!"

****

David returned some time later, his face shining, literally. His hair was dripping with – oil? He looked a little dazed as if he were attempting to figure out something. He ran his fingers through his hair, over his face and began to rub it into his hands and forearms. Their faces must have shown their own bewilderment at his state. Ari opened his mouth to speak.

"What has happened to you?" Ari got out before he was cut off.

"Do not ask," David replied, shaking his head. He brought his hands up and continued to smear the oil over his eyes and his whole face in a tired manner, indicating that he was overcome, overwhelmed and disbelieving all at the same time.

"You must tell us." Concern tinged Mal's voice. David's demeanor had him worried.

"Wooo," David sighed, blowing out a big breath. He didn't know where to pick up his story. "I'm not even certain … when I walked in, there was the *na-vee*," haltingly, he began, but that was as far as he got. The children suddenly peppered him with questions.

"The prophet?" Mal said.

"Where? Where is he?" Ari threw in.

"Tell us, SHOW us!" Martha pleaded, pulling on his arm, impatiently.

"Wait!" David shouted at their backs when they turned all at once, taking off in the direction of the house, leaving him behind.

Their minds were reeling. The young prophet was here? And he had done something to their friend, too! They wanted answers, they needed directions, but above all, they missed home. The prophet – he got them into this – he should be able to help!

They ran past the front gate, up the front path, through the courtyard, and were about to burst in as David had done, when good manners caught up to them. You don't just barge into a strange house, unannounced, they belatedly realized. They hesitated awkwardly at the front entrance, pondering what to do. David caught up to them as the door opened.

An old man, a really old man stood before them. Wizened and gray, he appeared truly wise and full of something akin to their prophet. But he was not their prophet, not the Young Master. This man was ancient. Their shoulders slumped in dismay and disappointment. He looked at them from shrewd eyes, nestled under stupendously bushy eyebrows which seemed to grow in every direction.

"Well, Jesse," the prophet said, "Who do we have here?" His voice, unlike his body, was strong.

"David?" A tall, commanding figure appeared behind the prophet, filling the doorway. He was older, but not elderly, like the prophet. He bore a strong resemblance to David. "You have company?"

"Yes, Father – I didn't get the chance to tell you." David said before the prophet broke in:

"Aha!" The older man raised one finger in the air, his mannerism suggesting he'd just figured out the answer to a riddle. "Not messengers." The prophet regarded them cannily, rubbing his chin. He put that one finger to his temple and cast his eyes upward as if he were seeking answers there. "But visitors," he finished solemnly, nodding his head sagely at David. "Hmph."

"Master Samuel, Father, these are my friends – Ari, Mal and Martha." David made the introductions.

"Don't let me keep you, young sire," the prophet interrupted. He turned to David with a slight bow. "I must get back for I've already tarried here too long." The children parted to let him leave. David grasped his arm and elbow, solicitously, to help him down the path. He could see a servant waiting near the main road with a donkey and cart, making preparations to transport Samuel to his next destination. As Samuel passed by, Ari stirred from his stupor long enough to realize: even though he wasn't *their* prophet, he still may be able to provide some answers.

"Can you help us?" Ari murmured as he mimicked David's actions, turning to grasp the prophet's other arm to assist him. He had a feeling that Samuel would understand his question without requiring further explanation.

"I imagine," the prophet turned to Ari and paused. He looked at Ari from beneath his wayward brow and wagged his finger at them all. "You all could get home in much the same manner in which you came."

Which really isn't an answer at all, Ari seethed. He considered the words of the prophet, and the thought came to him: *How was that helpful?* He was really getting tired of cryptic responses. But he remained silent, respectful of the age and station of the older man. As they continued down the walkway, Ari and David relinquished Samuel to the care of the servant who'd come to meet them. The servant helped the old prophet down the remainder of the path and into the cart while Ari and David hovered.

"Did you need help getting home?" David's father turned to Mal and asked, misunderstanding Samuel's comment. He was confused by the exchange. He thought Ari asked for a ride and Samuel had refused. But why would the prophet refuse to help?

"No, Father, they need to stay here." David responded quickly, just in time to save Ari from thinking of a reply. Truly, Ari didn't know what his response to David's father could be. What could he say? Yes, we do need help getting home? Or no, you can't help us? Ari knew if the prophet wasn't helpful, likely David's father would prove the same.

"Now, David," his father chided. His son had a habit of forming fast friendships.

"Father, they saved my life!" David interjected. "I owe them a debt."

"Very well," David's father raised his brow at that bit of news but held his peace regarding the revelation. His eyes promised that there would be more time spent on that subject later. He scrutinized them keenly for a long moment, looking each of them in the eye as he assessed them. They must have passed inspection, for he capitulated, immediately becoming the gracious host. "You are welcome in my home." He stepped back out of the doorway, gesturing with a sweep of his arm for them to enter.

Basins were provided to wash away the grime of travel, which the children thankfully accepted. They were all too ready to rid themselves of the grunge of their journey. Martha felt the dirt must surely be embedded in her skin by now but resisted the urge to give her feet a nice long soak. She joined Ari and Mal as they took their seats among David and his family.

That night, the children feasted as they had not in a long while, it seemed. Jesse treated them as honored guests. Roasted succulent meats were piled high and put before them, served along with *le-hhem* and savory dipping sauces. Olives, leeks, squash, onions and garlic rounded out their meal, followed by sweet figs and honey baked into cakes. They tried to mind their manners but fell on the food eagerly. It seemed that it had been longer than two days since they had a good, home cooked meal. Even though it wasn't their home, it made their own feel that much closer and eased some of their longing.

David's older brothers (all seven of them!) were called home for the occasion of the prophet's visit, so it almost seemed more like a holiday. The atmosphere was festive and jovial. The brothers really seemed to enjoy one another, appearing as though they hadn't seen each other in a while, or that they didn't know when they would see each other again. David joked and jostled with them as they called him "Lord David." He fended off their ribbing and good natured insults and countered with his own. Martha recognized the young man who'd come to deliver the message to

David yesterday morning. Eliab was his name she believed, and he was the eldest brother. He sat next to David, and the two of them carried on so much that she was nearly in tears laughing at them.

"So – you think he's funny, little one?" Eliab turned to her, all at once, including her in the joke. He scowled at her but Martha was laughing so hard, she couldn't find it in her to be repentant. She couldn't even muster a straight face. The two brothers were hilarious!

David's hair, still lustrous from the oil, began to fall over his face and get in his eyes throughout their meal. He blew at the locks, distractedly, time and again. Finally, he flung his hair back in frustration, to get it off his face altogether. The action made him look so regal that it drew another chorus of "Lord David." Before long, they had elevated him to king.

"If 'My Lord' can tear himself away from his fascination with his hair ..." Eliab began. David looked mortified at being caught, but his hand drifted up and touched his hair, self-consciously, fiddling with it.

"David, you will show our guests where to sleep?" his father broke in, changing the subject and diverting David's attention.

"Yes, *av*," David sobered, looking up expectantly. His father didn't speak much unless he had something to say. He knew more was coming. The other occupants of the table grew quiet when Father spoke.

"Tell me, *yadid* – how did you come to meet them?" Jesse inquired solemnly. The children's eyes widened, and they looked to each other. Ari gulped. David was about to answer, but his father continued, luckily for them. "And how is it that *you* came to be so far away from home?" They realized his father's accusations were directed at David, not them.

"Er …" David began. He scratched his head as he searched for an explanation. He tried for a conciliatory tone. "Abba, I know -"

"Don't 'Abba' me. I've told you, time after time. No more than a day's journey away from home. Your brothers shouldn't have to go so far to find you. Anything could happen." He gave David a meaningful look.

"But Abba, I can take care of myself!" David insisted.

"I know you can," his father agreed, "but I worry sometimes that you'll be so distracted by your musings, your writings, even your music that something or some animal may catch you unawares."

The children exchanged looks – that's sort of what happened! TWICE! David hung his head and looked guilty. Jesse read the looks on their faces.

"I know my son," he said to them, wryly, eyebrows raised. To David he added gently, "I don't want to *have* to worry about you, David. I want you to live long and grow to have your own family one day. I want to bounce your children on my knee. So, in the future, try not to stray so far from home," Father ended sternly.

"Yes, *av*," David answered meekly.

****

"He treats me like such a baby sometimes," David grumbled later. He was a little frustrated and humiliated at being rebuked in front of his friends. They gave him commiserating looks but privately, they were conflicted.

At that moment, Ari wished he could hear his mother calling him, "my lamb!" To think about his own father still hurt too much, so he purposely kept his thoughts from veering in that direction. Martha wished she could be safe in her home right now, where her father would tenderly tweak the nose she so detested as it was a replica of his own. And Mal just wished that his own father were around more often so he could spend more time with him. Right then, he missed his dad a lot.

"You have a great father," Mal said aloud, voicing his thoughts. He knew David's father corrected him out of love as any parent would. There was no need for embarrassment.

David looked past the vexing conversation with his father, sighed and agreed with Mal. As they sat around the fire contemplating the day's events, Martha's head began to nod. The light of the fire and the soft conversation, not to mention the roof over her head and a full stomach, all combined to lull her to sleep. She hadn't felt this cozy and comfortable, so secure and protected, in a while.

"Somebody's sleepy," David noticed she was drifting off.

"Sorry," Martha mumbled and yawned. "This just feels so nice."

"Bed for you," David replied and got up from his place in front of the fire. He felt good knowing his self-appointed mission to provide shelter and protection for his guests was now accomplished because Martha felt safe. He reached down to pull her to her feet and escorted her to his mother, who took Martha to his sister's old quarters to sleep in. David's sisters were married now and had moved away to begin families of their own.

When Martha saw the room, she initially balked at the idea of being separated from the boys, but David's mother ushered her inside, tsking and clucking when she would have turned away. Martha was too tired for strenuous objection anyway. She soon realized that it was kind of nice to be able to spend some time alone, in a girl's room, surrounded by feminine things. Surrendering to the gentle ministration of a mother's touch, she laid her head on the soft pallet and drifted off immediately into an exhausted, dreamless sleep.

Meanwhile, Ari and Mal waited for David to return. They still had unanswered questions. Since the prophet, Samuel wasn't *their* prophet, what was his reason for coming? They were curious as to what this had to do with David. They put the question to him upon his return.

"He said I was ..." David responded hesitantly to their query. He paused and shook his head as if he found it too incredulous to repeat. He tried again. "When he saw me, the prophet took out his horn of oil and poured it all over my head. He said I was anointed to be the next king." He stammered at this point in his story, his voice filled with wonder. "He said our God chose me out of all my brothers. Me!"

Ari and Mal exchanged a look. And then another. Mal's brows knitted together, and Ari's forehead creased as the final pieces of the puzzle fell into place. Disbelievingly, they thought: No, it couldn't be! Could it? Simultaneously, they both raised their eyebrows as realization dawned on them. Suddenly, it all made sense.

"What?" David caught their expressions.

"Oh, nothing," Ari said in his sing-song way, his voice went up an octave. He was so bad at lying.

"We were just thinking," Mal attempted to cover their slip up, "maybe we should call you 'lord' now?"

"Oh - please don't do that!" David objected earnestly. "I've already had to endure comments from my brothers all evening. 'Lord David' this and 'Lord David' that, all the bowing and scraping." He rolled his eyes, "Besides, it hasn't even happened, yet. You are my friends. To you, I'm still just David."

Chapter 21

Early the next morning, David awakened them, telling them he had an errand to run for his father. The house was curiously quiet, compared to the previous night. David explained that his three eldest brothers had left soon after dinner. They needed to return to battle, for only by the request of the prophet were they allowed to come home. Before leaving, they'd shared stories from the battlefront with their father that had him concerned. He now worried about them and wanted David to go, under the guise of taking provisions, to see about them.

His sons, Jesse knew, would see through the ruse and know he was checking on them. Eliab, Abinadab and Shammah, didn't need food already, for they had only been home the night before. Jesse felt some remorse, too, at chastening David in front of his friends and wanted to make it up to him. David was thrilled to be going "to war," even though, technically, he wasn't. He thought Mal and Ari might want to tag along, too. And, in no way could Martha be left behind. So David decided to take all of his friends with him.

It was a beautiful, bright day. Mal and Ari were strangely quiet at the thought of going, and they exchanged knowing looks. Martha, reunited with her lamb after a good night's rest, would actually have rather they left her behind, but she was resigned to staying with the group. She hugged Mary in goodbye and gave her little head a final pat as they prepared to depart. David left his flock in the care of his father's servants and harnessed the mule. Martha climbed aboard the oxcart, now hitched to the mule, while Mal and Ari helped David with the food. They loaded parched grain, loaves of bread and gifts of cheese for the captains into the oxcart. When they came to relieve David of his portion, she noticed, again, how oddly subdued Mal and Ari were. They were treating David differently and seemed to defer to him even more. What was their problem?

David was about to get into the cart when Samson appeared at his side. The big dog wagged his tail enthusiastically when he saw the oxcart, eager to take his place. But David vetoed that idea.

"Samson, no!" he commanded, when the dog tensed, preparing to jump aboard the cart. Samson gave David a questioning look and cocked his head to the side. "No," David said again, more sternly. "Go back. Besides," he added, "I don't have room for you." Samson looked pointedly at the remaining space in the cart, then back at David and whined in response.

"That's not for you. See?" He gestured to Mal and Ari as they laid the food into the wagon. Samson looked depressed, hung his head dejectedly, and slunk away. David stood there, hands on his hips, shaking his head at the retreating canine.

"Aw!" Martha said, feeling sorry for Samson. "He looks so sad!" Samson halted at Martha's tone, looking for sympathy. He gave David a hangdog expression.

David turned at Martha's comment, still shaking his head. "Don't feel too sorry for him. He always tries – right Samson?" Samson's ears perked up at the sound of his name. The dog looked at David hopefully, shaking his tail and taking a step in their direction. David held up his hand, "Now go on …" David made a little shooing gesture with his hands. Samson obeyed, but kept casting glances back at David, in hopes that his master would change his mind. Rolling his eyes at Samson's dramatic shenanigans, David strode to the front of the cart and hopped in. He took the reins from Mal, who sat up front. Their destination: The Valley of Elah.

****

Their journey to the site of battle was uneventful. As they reached the encampment, they saw the gnarled branches of the terebinth trees which marked the valley. David drew up and stopped the oxcart at a row of tents near the battlements. The camp was strangely quiet for a war to be going on, Martha thought. David leaped from the head of the cart and tossed the reins to Mal. Mal gave a nearly imperceptible bow, just a solemn lowering of his head, but Martha caught it.

"Never to me, my friend," David shook his head at Mal and threw his hands up, laughing as he backed away. He caught sight of Eliab, grabbed a basket of food from the back of the cart and jogged to meet him.

"What is going *on*?" Martha whispered, as soon as David left. She looked from Ari to Mal, puzzled by their behavior.

"Shhhh … just watch," Mal said.

"DOGS!" A voice suddenly boomed into the quiet. Martha jumped at the sound. The hills on each side of the valley formed a natural amphitheater and the voice seemed to bounce around, ringing across the field. "Will no man fight me?" The voice thundered as a huge figure strode onto the battlefield.

****

To say that he was a big man would be an understatement. He was a giant of a man; so big that the children had never seen a man of his magnitude – at least ten feet tall. And everything on him was of mammoth proportions, from his helmet and heavy scaled armor, down to his sandals and sword. He carried a huge spear and had a javelin slung from his shoulders, too. If that weren't enough to induce knee-knocking fear, he was covered in bronze – even down to his leg coverings. He walked cockily, dust pluming with each step, like a man sure of himself and puffed up with his own self-importance. To lend credence to that idea, he even had a shield bearer. He paraded up and down the enemy side of the field, the ground quaking beneath him as he mocked the soldiers from the opposing side. His taunts were met with silence.

"For forty days, I have issued this challenge: beat *me* and we will be your servants. But if *you* lose, you will be our servants," he bellowed. "Not a man among you has come forth – is there no one who will stand up to me? You call yourselves warriors. More like cowards!" He turned to the line of soldiers behind him and brayed, loud and long. The air was filled with their raucous laughter as they joined him, and it reverberated throughout the valley until they sounded like a chorus of hyenas. The giant turned around and spat on the ground. "Worthless dogs! You and the god you serve!"

David bristled at that last comment. Anger rose in him, swelling and growing to behemoth proportions as large as the gargantuan enemy soldier. *How dare he?* David thought, hotly. Worse than the insult to the armies of his brothers, was the affront to the Creator. How dare he defy the armies of the One True God?

David looked at the mighty men of valor all around him in expectation. Many wouldn't meet his eyes; those who did looked belligerent and defiant. Sure, they could challenge the giant but to what end? Not a man amongst them could defeat him one on one. And what purpose would it serve – just to die fighting a giant? It was suicide. Many of the men had families at home to think about. And, while some were brave enough to contemplate it, they wanted their sacrifice to count for something, to mean something. To die a pointless death, was senseless. Not to mention, if they failed, they would doom their brethren to certain slavery. No one wanted to make a deal with the giant that could affect so many people. It made them all look like cowards; in this, the giant was correct. David made a decision.

"I will fight him." He set his lips with grim determination.

Several heads whipped in David's direction.

****

"Are you insane?" Eliab grabbed David and pulled him aside. "Pay him no mind!" Eliab said to the inquisitive bystanders. To David he hissed, "What are you doing here? And who's watching Father's sheep? Do you think this is some sort of joke – to agree to fight a giant?" Eliab glared at David and spoke through clenched teeth, enunciating each word, "This is not a pretense, David – this is real! This is no place for your jokes." He turned on his heel and stalked away. David ran after him.

"Wait, El," David began. "Eliab," he tried again. "Brother!" The honorific made Eliab pause for a moment, but then he resumed his pace. "Hear me. I – I know I can do this!" David said, excitedly. "God has already prepared me for this – he's given me a plan! Would you just listen?" he finally called at Eliab's back.

"I'm warning you, David. I'm in no mood to play," Eliab called over his shoulder. David jumped in front of his brother and held him by the shoulders, forcing Eliab to halt his march and meet his gaze.

"You were there. You heard what the prophet said," David said somberly, looking his brother squarely in the eye. He calmed as he saw he had Eliab's attention. "What you don't know is that God has already shown me how to defeat him. I killed a lion and a bear in the woods while I was away this last time." He didn't mention the children's participation because he was convinced, now more than ever that they were sent to prepare him for this very event.

"Really?" Eliab's face looked comical in his disbelief.

"Truly," David replied simply. "He is big. He is a giant. But he is no bear or lion."

Eliab chewed on the corner of his lip while he contemplated his choices. Should he send David home to Father, reprimanded? Or could he trust that God was really with his little brother? Most important of all, was it right to put the fate of them all into the hands of a shepherd boy? His mind reeled at the possibilities. David could be right and then they would all be saved. But what if he were wrong? Worse yet, he would surely be killed in the process. He couldn't bear the thought of having to deliver that news to Father. The responsibility of such a weighty decision was too much for him. In the absence of their father and the prophet, both of whom would know what to do in this situation, he did the only thing he could do.

"Come on," Eliab said, resolutely. He grabbed David by the arm and began hauling him towards one of the tents.

"What? Yes!" David recovered quickly from his initial confusion, realizing he had won. "But where are we going?"

"To see Saul."

Chapter 22

The tent of Saul, King Saul, to be exact, was elaborate. Though Saul came from humble beginnings and grew up working in the fields of his father, he had become accustomed to his kingly pleasures. His tent was larger than the others, held more conveniences and was made of fine materials. You couldn't just walk into his tent, a fact they soon found out when they were stopped at the entrance by a soldier in full war regalia.

"State your business," the soldier sneered, looking down his nose at them. His armor was more refined than those of his fellow warriors. While their garb was simple, leather with bits of metal, his armor was indicative of his status as the king's man, more metal than leather. The soldier's helmet sparkled in the sunlight.

"We desire an audience with the king," Eliab said, respectfully.

"Yes, we need to speak with him," David seconded.

"Why?" the soldier asked. There was no use in taking that simple message to the king's second in command or advisors without having a reason. They would want to know why. He looked at them, seeing the resemblance and discerned they were brothers. They probably wanted something of no consequence – perhaps, to settle a family squabble. The king would not want to be bothered.

"We may have the solution to his problem," replied Eliab.

"Problem? What problem?" the soldier prodded.

"I AM GOLIATH!" the giant roared, right on cue. His voice rebounded off the rocks and was amplified, magnified many times over. "Are none of you man enough to fight me?" He shook his massive fist and stomped his gargantuan foot for added effect.

The ground seemed to shudder in response. The soldier bucked his eyes in alarm before schooling his features into a mask, seemingly unconcerned by the display.

"THAT problem," David said, becoming exasperated. Eliab shot him a look at his sarcastic response, but David's face was angelic, the picture of innocence and respect. Smart mouthed comments would not get them in to see the king and could only serve to aggravate the situation. But David was growing impatient with the soldier's games.

"Well, what is it you think YOU can do?" the soldier responded caustically, smirking at them both. He would not let this child, this kid, this boy, get past him now. David stiffened at the soldier's question. His mind raced, thinking about what he could do to create a big enough stir to draw the king's attention outside to them. They had to get past that soldier.

"Enough!" cried a voice from within the tent. "The king will hear them."

The soldier started in surprise but obediently stood to the side, pulled back the curtain and ushered Eliab and David into the presence of the king.

As they entered the body of the tent, David saw several men standing around. He assumed correctly that they were the king's advisors and generals. He also recognized the face of one of the soldiers he saw standing outside earlier. From the looks on all their faces, he gathered that this soldier had beaten him to it – what he had to say would not be news to the king.

"So," a man addressed David in a weary voice. David could tell he was tall, even as the man reclined upon his couch. He sat up, leaning over as he rubbed his temples, suggesting he had a headache. He seemed worn and exhausted from worry as he looked up at David. "You think you can defeat our giant, eh?"

The man stood to his feet and towered over David. This must be the king. It was widely reported that he was head and shoulders taller than his countrymen. And it was so – he was taller than any man David had ever seen, except for the giant. David bowed his head in a gesture of respect and knelt before the king. Rendered momentarily speechless, he swallowed hard and answered the king, formally.

"Let no man's heart fail because of Goliath. I will fight him," David said as he found his voice.

King Saul gestured for David to rise. When David got to his feet, the king clasped his hand on David's shoulder and looked him over as if he were measuring the man he would become. David stood straight and didn't shrink back from the intense scrutiny, nor the king's daunting height. If he appeared intimidated by the king's stature and examination, how would he convince them he was able to defeat a giant?

"That's big talk for such a young man," Saul replied, and then posed the question, "I have promised glory, honor, riches and the hand of my daughter to the man who can defeat Goliath. Yet no man has come forward. How can it be that you can do what all other men fear to do?"

"My boldness comes from God, not myself. With him, I can do anything." David then recounted what he had told Eliab. "When I was in the wilderness and guarding my father's sheep, my God delivered me from the claw of the lion and the paw of the bear. Goliath will be like nothing compared to them." He finished with confidence, looking earnestly at Saul to make sure he was being taken seriously.

Saul heard David out and fixed him with a hard stare while brooding on his dilemma. Dare he believe that their salvation lay in the hands of this young shepherd? Finally, the king nodded his head.

"Suit him up."

"Surely you can't mean –" One of the king's advisors began to sputter in protest.

"I can and I do." The king did away with his objections. "I will allow it."

"But ..."

The king held up his hand to halt further opposition. "Perhaps the Lord has provided and sent the lad just for this purpose." David drew himself up and puffed out his chest at "the lad" comment, wanting to appear more mature. "He says that God is with him – we shall see." The king continued, "Get him my own armor."

Chapter 23

Martha ran to catch up with Ari and Mal as they hurried after David and Eliab. They seemed intent on listening in covertly. They would look at each other from time to time and nod, which drove Martha nearly insane.

"What are you doing?" she kept asking. The only response she got was an urgent "*shhhhh!*" as they eased closer to David and his brother. "What is going *on*?" she whispered as David and Eliab went inside the tent.

"You'll see," said Mal.

"Just watch," Ari chipped in. They sidled as close to the tent as they dared, trying not to draw attention to themselves. They caught snatches of conversation from the raised voices within, not enough to make sense to Martha but enough for Mal and Ari to exchange goofy grins.

Soon David emerged from the tent in soldier's garb. He had on full battle armor, from head to toe. As it turned out, the king's armor was much too large for David. It clanked in some places as he tried to walk and hung limply at his sides. It caused him to move in a clunky fashion. Martha's eyes popped open when she saw him, and her jaw went slack. Mal and Ari must have mirrored her expression, for David took one look at them all, growled, and went back inside the tent.

"I look ridiculous!" David protested as he re-entered the tent. The armor, being made for a fully grown, tall man only served to accentuate the fact that he was neither. "I can't fight in this – I can barely move!" He held up one piece and wailed, "I don't even know what this is!" The armor jangled noisily as he turned for their inspection.

The king gave him a hard look. Then, to everyone's surprise, he agreed with David. The more disproportionate the odds, the more this was beginning to seem like something orchestrated from above. Maybe the lowly shepherd boy could, indeed, bring down the giant. Goliath wouldn't expect such a tactic – it might throw him off and unsettle him completely. It was foolishness, certainly, but it could be crazy enough to work.

David emerged from the tent once again – dressed this time, in his simple shepherd's clothing. He went to the brook, which ran nearby, and picked out five smooth stones. He dropped them in his pouch and turned to leave. Without looking at Martha, Ari or Mal, he squared his shoulders in a determined manner and marched toward the battlefield, his face set in unyielding lines. When Martha's jaw dropped this time, it was in horror.

"What is he *doing*?" Martha's voice rose an octave. She was tired of their secrecy. Mal and Ari

scrambled to find a position on a nearby ledge that
jutted out above the field, where they would have a
better view. Martha followed closely behind, and the
boys held out their hands to help her up, lifting her
slight frame easily. From overhead, she watched as the
soldiers parted the way for David. Some grasped his
arms and touched his shoulders and back as he passed.
The bleak looks they gave him showed that they were
resigned to his fate, giving the impression they knew
they were sending a willing lamb to slaughter. This
was either the most brilliant plan, or the most
foolhardy.

Eliab grabbed David, just before he stepped
onto the field, and hugged him close to his chest. "I
will not let him kill you," Eliab vowed, "no matter
what."

"You won't have to," said David, giving Eliab
what he hoped was a reassuring smile, which really
came off as a slight grimace. If his plan worked –

WHEN, he corrected himself – Eliab and everyone else would be able to go home safe.

"No!" Martha gasped, and she finally comprehended what was about to happen. "Oh my!" David intended to fight the giant! She shook her head furiously in denial, "No, no, no! This can't happen!" She looked from Ari to Mal. "We must help him!" Power flowed instantly to her hand and fiery sparks emitted from her fingertips. She drew back, prepared to aim at the huge figure in the arena.

"Wait!" Mal grabbed her arm quickly, pulling it down to her side, looking around furtively to see if anyone else saw the display. She opened her mouth to protest when Mal looked at Ari and gave him a look that said, *get her.* Ari covered Martha's mouth. Together, he and Mal pulled Martha, still struggling, away from the rocky ledge.

"Mmmmph," she tried unsuccessfully to speak against Ari's hand.

"Listen!" Mal set her feet on the ground, let her go, and stepped in front of her. He held up his finger and glared at her. Martha quieted for the moment, breathing hard. Ari released her mouth. "That's David. DA-VID!" Mal spoke through tight lips. He gave her a bug-eyed look to indicate that it should be obvious. "It's his destiny to fight!"

"DESTINY?" Martha yelled as her face contorted. Ari clamped his hand on her mouth again but took it away when she attempted to bite him. "What do you mean, destiny?" she hissed.

"Martha," Ari released her and tried to reason with her. He held out the nearly bitten hand in a placating gesture. "I know David is our friend -"

"Yes, he is our friend, all the more reason to help him!" Martha broke in, near hysteria.

"But he is also *King* David," he continued, dismissing the interruption.

"The Warrior King," Mal interjected, impatiently. Martha looked at him blankly, still. Ari fished around for a way to explain that she would connect with. Mentally snapping his fingers, it came to him.

"The Beautiful King?" Ari tried again – he danced about a bit and shuffled his feet. If she didn't get it this time, he was out of adjectives.

"Ohhhhh!" Her eyes grew big. "Ahhhh … Hmmm …" Her face changed expression with each utterance. The pieces finally clicked in place for Martha as the full weight of what must have happened fell on her. Her head went a little woozy as she tried to process that bit of information. This was *David*, David! THE David, which could only mean that, somehow, they had been sent back in time! They were about to witness something that had already happened.

"Why didn't you just tell me that earlier?" Martha demanded.

"We weren't absolutely sure until now," said Ari.

"And we're about to miss everything while we explain it to you!" Martha was still dazed by their revelation and didn't even know whether Ari or Mal had said that. They were both jumping up and down, clearly aggravated, excited and wanting to get on with it. Martha glared at them suddenly as if they had both lost their minds.

"What are we waiting for? Let's go!" Now Martha was impatient, too. She could wait until later to digest everything. She pushed them in the direction of the ledge. They hurried to scramble back up the rocks, pulling her up as they went.

"But I'm warning you," she said as they regained the top. She looked down at her hand, which flickered in response. "He'd better not hurt David."

Chapter 24

David strode onto the battlefield, oblivious to the many pats he'd received from his fellow soldiers as he walked by. He thought of Eliab and his pending nuptials and resolved that he would send his brother home in peace. He thought of his father and remaining brothers. What would it mean for his family if they were reduced to servitude? For his nation? The more he brooded, the more determined he became. His focus was razor sharp. He would not lose.

The field seemed almost like an arena, fortified by hills and flanked by the armies on both sides. The giant, more mountain than man, was so busy bragging, boasting and putting on a performance for his fellow soldiers that he didn't notice David immediately. David seemed so insignificant on the vast plain; he was dwarfed in Goliath's shadow. The grating laughter of the enemy soldiers died down as David came into their view. Their eyes ran up and down the length of him, astonished that this would be the opposing side's answer to Goliath's challenge. Goliath gradually noted their response and turned to see the object of their attention. When his glance fell on David, he looked incredulous, then, fury slowly lit his features.

David had to lean back to look at Goliath, who was so big that his head blocked the glare of the sun from David's vision. But when the giant moved, the sun nearly blinded David with its intensity. He shielded his eyes with his hand, squinting into the bright sun. It gave him an idea. David loaded his sling.

Mal, Ari and Martha, watched in tense anticipation from their perch on the rocks. Even though they knew the supposed outcome, they found it hard to not interfere. What if they had done something that caused the events to change? Martha wrung her hands and held her breath. For a moment, she wished Samson was there to bite that old giant. She identified with David in that she knew what it was to feel small and insignificant, but that was where the similarity ended. Never had she ever faced such seemingly insurmountable odds. Although David did look diminutive in comparison to the giant, just then, he had never looked more beautiful. His bravery only added to the effect.

In contrast, Goliath looked downright disreputable. It seemed Martha could see the spittle fly from his mouth as he spoke, even from her vantage point. His thunderous speech slurred as if something were wrong with his mouth. And, indeed, there was. Teeth that protruded way past his lips were broken and chipped. A long scar ran down the length of his face, evidence of some poor, brave soul who got close enough, but had likely met his end in the attempt. Arms too long and disproportionate for his body came to their inevitable conclusion of gargantuan fingers, knobby and misshapen. He had massive legs like tree trunks. He didn't stand tall and erect, like David, but instead hunched his shoulders, which suggested he was used to stooping forward all of his life. Also, he *looked* really smelly, Martha thought to herself, hoping all the while that David didn't get close enough to confirm her hunch.

"Goliath has been a fearsome warrior ever since his youth," Saul had warned earlier. But David exuded confidence as he stood his ground and faced the giant. He, like Martha, weighed his enemy. He looked at the giant's physique and saw how he lumbered about. By no means was he built for speed. Yes, David was smaller, but he was also *faster*. Spirit came to him as it had so many times when he was alone with his sheep, encouraging and comforting him. It washed over him, bathing him and fortifying him. Suddenly, David knew he was not alone on that battlefield. He felt it in the breeze upon his hair, in the tingling along his spine, and in his readiness for battle.

"The Lord, *My God*," David murmured to himself. The Great Shepherd was with him. He shifted his feet on the sandy plain. Martha also felt it, this spirit, stirring. *Destiny*, it whispered. It was at that moment, she began to feel more than hope. Like Mal and Ari, she now *believed*. The boys, for their part, rubbed their hands and exchanged expectant looks – they were about to witness one of the greatest confrontations in history, right NOW.

Eliab, too, made ready. He was poised to rush in to save David should this turn out to be a fool's errand instead of the providence of God. He might perish in the attempt, but he could not allow his *ahh* to be slain. This could very likely be a suicide mission. If anyone was going to die, it should be him, allowing David to go free. He didn't relish the thought of carrying news of David's death to their aging father. It just might break him. Instead, David would be able to testify to their father that Eliab had died an honorable death.

But David was supremely aware that his God was with him. Just as God had always been with him and always helped him. David rested on that assurance. He had no doubt now that all the recent events in the woods, from the strange children he'd befriended to the attacks from wild beasts, were to prepare him for such a time as this. Despite Eliab's concern, he knew he would not die this day. His chin lifted a little higher.

"DOGS! Sons of dogs!" Goliath spat at the enemy's sidelines, refusing even to acknowledge David. "You send a boy to me? You insult me! Have you run out of men?" He shook his great fist as he taunted the battle line, overlooking David completely. His fellow soldiers jeered, spurring him to more antics. They filled the crude stadium with their guffaws. Goliath turned his back on David, deciding to treat him as if he were no more annoying than a fly. The boy, he sneered mentally, was no threat to him.

"Leave them alone!" David shouted fearlessly at the giant's back.

"You dare even speak to me? You gnat, you fly, you flea? I'll kill you and feed you to the vultures!" the giant bellowed over his shoulder. Enough! He would not be mocked. He'd teach the boy to make a fool of him. Turning, he reached for David, swatting at him, just as he would at a truly pesky insect. The shepherd boy saw the giant's hand coming towards him, like the paw of the bear, and nimbly dodged. "Hunh?" Goliath grunted, confused when his "fly" did not present himself for immediate squelching. But David was behind the giant, once more. The boy began to swing his sling overhead, building up momentum.

"How dare YOU insult our God?" David shouted at Goliath's back, undaunted. His voice swelled and grew with each word, being imbued with power and authority. "I come to you in the name of the Lord of Hosts, who helped me to kill both bear and lion. This is His battle. I will kill YOU. I will cut off *your* head. And I will feed *you* to the vultures so that everyone will know that our God *is* God!" David goaded the giant.

Enraged, Goliath turned again, falling for the ploy. This time the sun was in his face, momentarily blinding him. The giant reared back as the sun caught his eye, unknowingly mimicking the same pose as the lion. David saw his chance and ran at the giant at breakneck speed. Leaping, he landed on a boulder, and then pushed off the rock to gain more height. David hurled the sling while airborne. The smooth stone flew and found a home deep in the giant's forehead. It landed with a great THWACK! A stunned expression bled over the giant's features. His eyes rolled up, following the point of pain as if he were trying to see the stone now imbedded between his eyes. Then, Goliath toppled like a tree. He hit the ground with a thud that resounded across the valley and the huge mound of his flesh rippled with aftershocks.

The tumult from the enemy sidelines suddenly ceased as they saw their great champion fall. They stood there, stupefied while David stood over the fallen giant. The silence was deafening. Soaring on adrenaline and endowed with supernatural strength, David removed Goliath's own sword from the bronze scabbard. He hefted it up, holding it aloft in the air. The weapon glistened as it caught the sunlight. Martha watched the swift descent of the sword and turned her head, for she knew what was coming. Cheers erupted on their side, and she knew Goliath was well and truly dead.

"He did it! He did it!" The children shouted, jumping up and down. Their cries, a mixture of joy and relief, were soon drowned out completely by the shouts of victory down below them. They rushed down from their perch, thinking to greet David as he emerged from the arena. But it was not so easy for them to reach their champion. Eliab, however, was closest in proximity and managed to get to his little brother first. He ran on the field with a great whoop of joy, grabbing David and swinging him around. Relief was evident in his celebration. His brother was saved. They were all saved.

Chapter 25

Many of the soldiers surged forward in pursuit of the retreating enemy. The remaining crowd hemmed David in on all sides as they thronged about him, lifting him on their shoulders and celebrating their hero. The children fought to penetrate the crowd but soon found themselves pressed with their backs against the wall of rock.

That's when Martha saw him. Or rather felt him, watching them. She felt compelled to look in his direction and inhaled sharply. Eerie, golden-green eyes, like those of a cat, peered back at her. They looked strangely familiar, yet out of place as they were set in a man's face. He leaned casually on their oxcart, just on the opposite side of the crowd and stared lazily at her. He was incredibly handsome, with a face impossible in its perfection and dark, curling hair. He smiled at her – it was a beautiful smile – still, there was something off about him. He oozed malevolence; it rolled off of him in waves and screamed at her: HAVE NOTHING TO DO WITH THIS MAN! As if he were aware of her thoughts, his eyes suddenly flared and glowed luminescent, like those of a night predator, staring out at her from his man's face. And she was his quarry.

Mal and Ari didn't know what was going on, but they felt her reaction. Martha had gone quiet and still, like an animal about to bolt. She sensed danger. They looked to see what her eyes had found. The strange man straightened, indolently, and began to make his way easily through the crowd in their direction. The people seemed not to see him, but parted before him, avoiding him. The stranger moved fluidly, inhumanly, appearing to glide through them.

"No!" Martha breathed, suddenly panicked. She instinctively knew all was not well with the strange man. She clenched her fists to her chest and prayed, "Please – don't see us!" Martha closed her eyes, and moisture gathered together from the previously dry and arid atmosphere. Cloud formed out of the air, now humid, about them. It enveloped them in mist, hiding them from prying eyes. The smoky white substance formed an impenetrable barrier, camouflaging and sealing them against the rock. They couldn't see without nor could they be seen from within. They could only hear.

The stranger halted his approach, his eyes searching, for the children had all but faded into the background. Concealed from the outside world, they appeared to be part of the rock face. Invisible to him, he knew. *Click*, went the sound of his teeth as they snapped, biting at the air in frustration. He knew what had happened, but he was powerless to stop it.

A clenched fist went to his mouth, and he looked about him, looking for something to grab, throw, anything! He'd missed his opportunity. They were gone to him now – disappeared. Just the thought made his face momentarily contort with rage. He ground his perfect teeth in aggravation. He was about to lose his composure altogether when another thought occurred, calming him. His fist relaxed, and he smiled that beautiful smile. Time was on his side. He would get another chance. He only had to wait.

"We *will* meet again," he promised himself and them. Then, he too, vanished.

Martha, Ari and Mal stayed that way for some time, motionless and barely breathing, hidden in their cocoon of safety. They heard the procession of the crowd as they carried David away; their cries faded into the evening and silence followed. When she felt safe, Martha lifted the veil of cloud to find they were all alone. The battle ground and surrounding area were now deserted. The crowd was gone and David with them. It was eerily quiet. The mule, oxcart and empty tents were the only evidence that remained. All the victors were gone to celebrate or in pursuit of their enemies. The children had been left behind.

Martha stirred first. "We have to go find David," she said. He would be wondering what had happened to his companions.

Ari and Mal looked at her questioningly.

"We have to find David," Martha insisted, frowning at them. She made off in the direction of the oxcart before Mal pulled her back.

"Martha," Mal began gently, talking to her as he would, Hannah. "Our time here is finished." She gave him a confused look.

"Don't you see?" Ari added, "We did what we came to do. We helped David."

"Right," said Mal. He felt, he sensed it. Just as he'd trusted Martha's instincts about the strange man, he knew now he could trust his own. "We have no place here, in this time. We don't belong here."

"Our place is home," Ari finished.

Martha didn't look convinced. "But he's going to need us! He'll need our help again!" she protested, remembering some of the stories about David, the Warrior and Beautiful King, and the trials he would face. At least they could warn him of some of the obstacles and keep him from making grievous errors. Her face took on a stubborn look; there was an obstinate lift of her chin. Mal recognized that look. He'd seen Hannah display it too, many times. Martha wasn't budging.

"Martha, we need to find home," Mal persisted. But Martha looked away, down the road, in the direction she hoped to find David.

"But he needs us," she said in a small voice. "He's our friend," Martha's lip trembled and tears sprang to her eyes. She wavered, torn between the desire to be back at home and of a mind to follow David. "What will happen to him without us?"

"We already know how his story ends, Martha," Ari responded. "He lives a long life and makes some major mistakes –" Martha looked alarmed at that.

"BUT, overall, he was a good king," Mal rushed to cover swiftly for Ari, giving him a warning look. No need to get her riled up again.

"If we stay, we can make sure he doesn't make those mistakes," Martha wheedled. She looked hopeful for a moment, then crestfallen. Her shoulders sagged. "But those are his mistakes to make. Mother says that our mistakes help us to grow into the people we're to become."

"Maybe he's meant to make those mistakes," said Ari, coaxing gently. "We're not supposed to be part of his world – otherwise the stories would say, David and Mal and Martha and Ari." He smiled at his own joke.

Martha looked resigned as her practical side won out, but she dragged her feet anyway while they walked toward the cart.

"Besides," Ari concluded, "who knows what damage we could do if we stay? We could change the world in *our* time." He rubbed his hands together briskly indicating that was the end of the matter. "Now that's settled – how do we get back?" He stood with his hands on his hips and looked from Mal to Martha, expectantly.

Mal shrugged helplessly and scratched his head. He hadn't figured that part out yet. Though the valley was already ancient in their time, Mal looked about him for a landmark that could somehow confirm their location. "This place looks as though it *might* be familiar – maybe we're actually not too far from home." Two vague statements were joined together, he knew, but Mal was determined to be optimistic. "If we could only get back to the beach, where it all started, we could figure out how to get home?" He tried hard not to end on a question, but he really wasn't sure it would work.

Ari agreed with Mal – he thought it seemed like a good place to begin. They could try following the brook where David had retrieved the stones. Maybe it would lead to a body of water they would recognize. At least, now they had a plan. And transportation, they realized. The boys turned and headed, once again, towards the cart, which was forgotten during the celebration. Martha sighed heavily and stared glumly down the road, in the opposite direction of where the boys were headed. She squinted her eyes in the fading light and craned her neck for signs that David had returned for them.

Finally giving up on that notion, she called abruptly at their backs, "It's intent!" She surrendered the information grudgingly. It nearly burst from her as if she were compelled to say it.

"What?" Mal halted, one foot already in the cart. Ari paused as he grabbed the reins. They turned to look at Martha in unison.

Exasperated, Martha threw up her hands. It seemed she was the only one who was paying attention. She tried to explain again when they looked bemused.

"Haven't you even asked yourselves the question why? Why here? Why this place – with him?" She queried. Mal and Ari continued to look at her blankly. She cast her eyes heavenward.

"I've been asking myself those questions ever since you told me who he is!" She shook her head and tsked at them, reveling for a moment. Now she knew something that they didn't know. She savored the knowledge, a sweet payback for them holding back about David's identity.

"Get on with it, already!" Ari said impatiently, frowning. Then his expression cleared as he thought

222

about her questions. Martha gave him a smug look. "Oh!" His eyebrows lifted as he recalled. "We were play fighting and talking about how we wish we could have been here."

"We wanted to meet the Warrior King," Mal said in a hushed voice, filled with awe. "Somehow, we did this, we created this." The implications of what they had achieved staggered his mind - incredible! "But how?" He still looked confused.

"Well, as near as I can figure," Martha responded, "we were all thinking about the same thing at the same time. Someone even mentioned moving back in time! The catalyst was when I touched you both as I fell." She was talking excitedly now, more sure of her theory.

Ari was still stuck on *catalyst*. Where did she get such a word? Mentally, he rolled his eyes. Martha needed to get out more. Clearly, she spent way too much time around adults.

"So," Mal said slowly as he was finally able to grasp the significance of those events, "If we all think about home and touch each other, with the intention of getting home, we should be able to get back there?" Martha nodded in response, her hair bobbing happily. "Brilliant!" Mal beamed.

"Wait – what?" Ari blurted. He shook his head and caught up to the conversation. "Never mind, I'm ready!" he said and held out his hand.

"Me, too!" Mal's hand joined Ari's. They both held out their hands to Martha, palms up. "We can't do this without you," They looked at Martha. She gave Mal her hand, then Ari.

"Of course, you can't," she sighed in agreement. "Let's go home." No sooner than she said those words, darkness fell.

Chapter 26

The Beach … finally

It was pitch black for a moment. Well, not exactly – light stemmed from a single spot. The pinprick of light seemed to glow in the distance. It swelled and grew larger as if it were coming toward them, getting closer. No, it appeared that they were going towards the light, on second thought. They heard sounds they well recognized that seemed to be coming from a sea shore – waves lapping, birds crying. As they drew closer, the illumination spread until the scene unfurled before them like an immense painting, filling their entire field of vision. The smell of the sea and the sand underfoot was more than memory. It was real. They were back at the beach, at the spot where they last stood, under the bright midday sun.

A seagull squawked and drew their attention. They turned their heads to find The Young Master, not far from where they stood. He stooped and added a few pieces of wood to his fire, where fish baked over the open coals. The smell was delectable, they thought, suddenly realizing they were all hungry. As when they had left, the beach was deserted.

As the children started towards him, he looked up, all at once, encompassing them in his steady gaze. They heard his voice say to them, clearly, resounding in their heads.

"Now, knowing what you know, and all it entails, would you still say yes?" His voice was gentle. An answer was required, but he would not use compulsion. They realized that he was giving them a choice. They could still back out, even now. The children hesitated. What would happen if they turned away from their gifts?

"*Sha-khahh,*" the answer came to them on a whisper and they knew. They would simply forget. The word already whipped at their memories, tugging at its tendrils, tempting. For Mal and Martha, it would be as if they'd never met Ari. They only need surrender to the suggestion, and they could all return to life as they knew it. Their journey would be undone.

But looking at each other, they realized the bonds had already been formed. Friendships forged in fire, by trials and in shared secrets. Even measuring what they had been through, would they do it again? Ari looked to Mal and raised one eyebrow, Mal looked to Martha and she grinned. How could they go back now? Without a doubt, they knew their answer: *Yes!*

Joyfully, they ran to the Young Master. Martha leaped into his outstretched arms. Ari and Mal crowded in, too. They were home at last.

The Young Master set Martha down on her feet. He looked into her eyes with that, now familiar, twinkle. Feeling shy and in awe of his presence, Martha cast her eyes down under his scrutiny. The boys, too, were suddenly reserved. They all stood, heads bowed, reverent. But, the Young Master put his finger under her chin, bringing her face up to meet his eyes, once again.

"So," he smiled at her, "had a bit of an adventure, did we?" He took her finger and twirled her around, as indulgent as any father. "None the worse for wear," he added, looking them all over from head to toe. He winked at Martha. She grinned so hard, her ears hurt and her face felt like it was splitting. She was really happy to be back home, but inexplicably, even more so to see him. He filled her with joy.

Mal and Ari had goofy grins, too. But they recovered before Martha and began to regale the Young Master with the account of their escapades. The children shared in his simple meal, which was unaccountably good. The fish was as delectable as it smelled. And it tasted heavenly – flaky, moist, charred in all the right places and perfectly seasoned. Mal and Ari acted out the scenes of their exploits animatedly and in great detail, illustrating how Martha first got her power and saved David from the bear. Eventually, they shared how they got their own powers and finally, how David killed the lion, the bear and Goliath. They talked about how they met David and didn't even realize who he was for a few days.

"Speaking of, what day is this anyway?" Ari wanted to know how long he was gone. He thought of his mother and wondered how worried she must have been. The same thought occurred to Mal and Martha simultaneously. If they all missed home, surely their parents must have missed them.

"It is still the same day you left; it has only been a short while that you've been gone," The Young Master answered. "All is as you have left it. Only you have been changed." He was met with scrunched faces as they tried to comprehend how that could be possible. Their faces relaxed as they gave up and accepted his answer, realizing they didn't need to understand exactly what happened any more than they had to understand time travel. It was a relief to Mal and Martha that all was the same. Ari, however, felt differently.

"*Rabboni*," he began, stepping forward hesitantly, "now that I," he looked at the others, "*we* can travel back in time – can I see my father?" That question had been burning in him, ever since he knew it was David, the warrior king of old. Ever since he realized what it could mean for him. Things had been hard for him, he and his mother, since Father died. Ari would dearly love to see him, again, just once.

"Well," the Young Master seemed to consider Ari's question and the possible ramifications before he answered. "The problem with that is, once would not be enough. It's never enough. To let go of a loved one is hard, but their time here is over. Your time has only just begun. You would be there, in the past, trying to recapture that life. But I need you to live your life, the life you are destined to live, here and now." Ari nodded and swallowed. It was not what he'd hoped to hear, but he tried to accept it.

"I do have one question," Martha began, shyly. She had been silent until this point, waiting for a chance to interject her perspective. Her companions had been so boisterous in their retelling of the tale that she had restrained herself, content merely to bask in the presence of the Young Master. "Before we left, there was a man. He was strange and frightening." She described their encounter with the man and the feelings he invoked, like she should run or hide. The Young Master nodded as she spoke, as though her words confirmed what he already knew.

"Martha, you did well. You paid attention to your instincts, which is good. My spirit is always with you and will guide you if you allow," he said, encouragingly. "As for the strange man, you were wise to avoid him. He is your adversary. He seeks to destroy all things that are good. He prowls about like a lion that wants to devour you. He wants you, but he cannot have you. That doesn't mean he won't try." He gave them all a penetrating look. "Where there is unrest, confusion, dissension and any sort of evil work afoot, you will find him."

Martha's head bobbed in agreement. That made sense. He felt all wrong, like evil, personified. And now, he was after them. The thought unsettled her.

"Do not be worried, Martha," said the Young Master. He clasped her chin and turned her face up to meet his eyes. "He cannot have you. I have good plans for you, remember? Have courage and have faith!"

The Young Master touched her shoulder and Mal and Ari's in turn. "It is time for you to go home now. Your families will soon be wondering where you are." He held up his hand when they opened their mouths to protest. They had more to tell him, more questions to ask him about their powers. "Don't worry. More will be revealed to you in time. All I need to know now is that you are willing to serve."

"I am!" they chorused.

"Good. You will see me again, when I have need of you. Meanwhile, if you have need of me, just call my name." As the young prophet turned away from them, a mist appeared on the ground that quickly enveloped him.

"But," Ari stepped forward to ask the obvious question. "What is your name?"

"Yes," Mal appealed to his retreating back, "what should we call you?"

For a moment, they thought they would receive no answer. Then his voice carried back to them, resonating across the mist.

"I am called *Yeshua.* I am known by many other names, as well ... Emmanuel, Counselor, Prince of Peace, Alpha and Omega. But you may simply call me ... *friend.*"

Chapter 27

Ari

... reached home in the fading light. By now, his mother would surely be worried. He quickened his steps. As he walked into their home, his mother stood there, hands on her hips. Her face was turned down in a disapproving scowl, which quickly turned to relief when she saw him. She wasn't used to him being away from home for so long.

"Ari, where have you been?" She started in on him immediately.

"Mom," Ari began, but she cut him off. She was a little worked up, so he let her go at him for a while.

"You had me worried! I was about to send your uncle looking for you – it's just not like you to be gone all day." She had to say her piece, just to get it all out of her system. Ari waited patiently for an opening.

"Mama, listen!" he said when she paused for breath. "Mama – I made friends today!"

"Friends?" she said, emphasizing the s. Plural, as in, more than one. Intriguing.

"Yes, Mama," Ari replied.

"Real friends?" she teased, brought back to her customary good humor. She was comforted knowing that her son was not alone anymore.

"Yes, Mama!" he stomped his foot, just a little, in protest. She was making fun of him.

"True friends?" This time, Mama wasn't teasing. She needed to know that his friends were of the sort she'd like him to have.

"Yes, Mama," he said, indulgently. She opened her arms for a hug and was taken by surprise. Although she didn't know it, he gave her three days' worth of hugs. He'd really missed her.

"I'm so happy for you, my lamb!" She said, as she gathered him into her arms. There was that pet name again – but this time, he just didn't mind.

****

Martha

… climbed up to the roof of her home, into a full assemblage of her mother's "company." They weren't really company in the true sense of the word – really more like family. Her mom had decided to have a gathering to celebrate her baby sister's weaning. Martha shot past her family, weaving through bodies and calling for her mother as she moved. When she found her, she slowed and walked into her arms. She didn't want to alarm her mother. She wrapped her arms around her mother's waist and looked up into her face. But she didn't cry. She wouldn't. She just wouldn't let her go.

Mother looked down at Martha, searching her face. She gave her daughter a keen, discerning look through narrowed eyes. Her face showed the beginnings of a frown, and she was about to ask Martha if all was well.

"*Shalom Ima*," Martha replied at the questioning look. She reassured her mother that everything was fine. Just then, Martha felt a little tug on the hem of her garment. Distracted, she turned to see her baby sister, one hand fisted into Martha's clothing, the other outstretched as though she wanted to be picked up. Martha swooped the toddler up into her arms, laughing. Her little sister, Mary, giggled in response.

Little Mary followed Martha around for the rest of the night, wanting to be near her, begging for her touch. To Mary, it seemed, Martha really had been gone for three days. With the older siblings home to help mother, Martha was free to find a little corner and fall asleep. She woke up with Mary stretched across her torso and smiled.

"Mary was a little lamb ..." she sang softly to herself. She stroked her little sister's hair, softer than the wool of her own pet lamb, yet, somehow reminiscent. It was good to be home.

****

Mal

... was greeted by the sight of Hannah's back as he came through the doorway. She turned to look at him accusingly, and then turned her face back to the wall. He could tell that she had been crying; grimy tear tracks ran down on each side of her face.

"Hannah," Mal went to her immediately, crouching next to her. "What is wrong? Why are you crying?"

She looked at him, pouted and sniffed, for full effect. Mentally, he rolled his eyes but played along for her sake. Hannah was such an actress.

"You said you would tell me a story," she responded, looking forlorn and sounding altogether pitiful. "But when I waited for you, you didn't come back and then you took ALL DAY!" she wailed, giving him a baleful look.

"Is that all?" Mal teased, poking her in the tummy with his finger. He gathered her up into his arms. She didn't resist. Hannah knew when she had won. Her big brother was about to make it all better. "Do I have a story to tell you ..."

Epilogue

"And my friends? What of my friends?" David inquired. After all the excitement had died down and the celebrations were ended, David looked for his companions. They were nowhere to be found. He asked of Eliab, and many of the men who were there, but all he received in reply was a shake of the head.

David went back to the site of his victory to retrieve his father's mule and wagon. He had to see for himself that his friends were not there, looking for him. Waiting for him. He found the animal, still attached to his harness, and only shouting distance away from the battle ground. The mule was none the worse for being left alone for a day or so and had found food to eat in the nearby patches of grass. But there was no sign of Ari, Mal or Martha.

David then perceived that what he'd originally thought was true: The Lord had sent messengers, helpers, to prepare him for the battle with Goliath. Though sad that he would not see his friends again, he rejoiced in the knowledge that God had taken care of him as he had known all along. He climbed up into his father's wagon, gathered the reins and gave them a flick to encourage the mule.

As the cart headed towards home, David began to sing softly to himself:

> *The Lord is my Shepherd,*
>
> *I shall not want …*

Glossary

Adonai – Lord

ahh – brother

a-hhot – sister

av, Abba - father, papa

ba-yit - house

bo – come

bor – cistern

eym, Ima – mother, mommy

na-vee – prophet

patér – father (Greek)

qa-rav – come near

Rabboni - Master

seh – lamb

tey-vah – vessel

yadid - beloved

About the Author

My background includes Sunday school teacher, women's bible study leader, public speaker, choir director and soloist. I'm the mother of two children, both now adults. Raised the daughter of a Baptist minister, I have followed his legacy and created several ministries that flourished – bible study, praise team and singles ministries. I'm a great fan of the Bible and love to tell my versions of the stories found therein. At the urging of my friends, I began to write a blog, *The Word in My Life*, to encourage others by applying the scriptures to my life events. I'm so excited about the release of the first book in the *Touched* series because it allows me to combine my love of young adult literature, fantasy adventure, AND stories from the Bible. I can't wait to share more journeys of Ari, Mal and Martha with my fans!

The song of David in Chapter 13 is a paraphrase of Psalm 8 as found in the Good News Translation. All italicized words in the Glossary are ancient Biblical Hebrew unless otherwise noted.

Made in the USA
Charleston, SC
06 July 2015